I0683238

CORRUPTION

TAYLOR HONDOS

Print ISBN : 978-1-927940-83-9
EPUB ISBN : 978-1-927940-84-6

This is for all the dreamers out there.

PART ONE
Prologue: Gabe
Three Months Ago

THERE WAS NO one around for miles; a desolate place where there were no survivors. No fighters. There would be none by the end of this. I knew this, and the world most certainly knew this.

I landed with a thud, and looked around out of habit to see if anyone had heard the sound. Of course they hadn't though, no one cared, and there was no one left to hear. I squinted my eyes trying to grasp an image in the dark ahead of me. Finally as my eyes adjusted, I could see him. His eyes watched me from afar, unmoving. I waited. When I saw he wasn't moving an inch from his place, I sighed deeply. *He is going to make me walk the whole way to him,* I thought anxiously.

I trudged forward slowly, milking it. Each clunk underneath me felt like a hammer slamming down on my back. *Ha, Going to make you wait for me.* If he wanted me to walk this whole way, then he was going to have to wait up on me.

She was heavy in my arms. Dead weight. Her eyes were closed, and her mouth was slightly ajar. She was in a deep sleep. That was for sure. I examined her forehead. It was black, with dried up blood all around it. The rot was deep, and I didn't know how she would ever be useful again. He wanted her though. She was the main part of this operation. I turned away from the rot before I felt ill. I had done this. I had caused her to rot so severely.

I wondered how Jared ever got so close to her. It was pretty gruesome being this close to her. Her head slumped over to the side in response to my thoughts. I held her as best as I could until I reached him.

"I see you brought the girl with you." He spoke through the silence as a greeting to me. He turned away from me and began walking in the other direction. I rolled my eyes. *Seriously? Do I have to carry her the whole damn way? I should throw her on the ground; maybe then he would pick her up.*

"How'd you pull that off?" he said calmly. I smirked, but it was followed by a grunt as I tripped over my own feet. *Idiot.*

"Well, Jared thinks she was lying just as we planned. I gave her the "antidote" but remember its effects are only for three hours." He stopped sharply, causing me to trip again, and scowled at me.

"And?" He questioned as I sighed at the disapproval in his voice.

"Well, the plan was to inject her with even more of the disease. Remember?" I sarcastically added. This was his plan, after all. He should have known it.

He simply stared at me. I felt like an idiot, so I went rambling on.

"I mean, I gave her the full dosage while she slept." He simply scowled. Lena was getting heavier by the minute. I grunted as I could feel myself losing grip of her and I heaved her up. He scowled and turned quickly away from me as he continued to walk on and I nearly growled in frustration.

There was silence for another minute as we walked on. All that could be heard was our footsteps on the deserted land. "And?" he said again, finally stopping his footing for what I hoped would be the last time. We were in an open field.

"See for yourself." I frowned at him more out of the weight I was carrying than my frustration. He looked down to her finally. He was silent for a moment, but then he smiled. The biggest smile I had ever seen him make was erupting on his face. It was almost creepy how happy he was from seeing someone who looked as frightening as she did.

"She's sicker than I thought she would be. You have done your job well." He nodded in approval. He finally pulled her from my arms and into his own. I felt instant relief in my aching arms. He began walking away, leaving me standing there, dumbfounded.

"What about our deal?" I shouted after him cautiously, but firmly.

"The deal will be in place, when you bring her to me too." I froze, and I felt my blood boiling, but I had to keep my cool on the outside. My heart was pounding and breaking at the exact same time. My breathing was restricted in my throat, and I gasped for air. I hoped he didn't notice.

"Holland is out of this." I said as calmly, and as nonchalant as I could say it.

"She's been in this ever since she started injecting those people with the disease." He said simply, while throwing up his hand to dismiss me. End of conversation, but it wasn't over for me.

"Unknowingly," I added quickly. He held my gaze for a long while, making the air around me seem thick. I was getting sweaty palms. He was on to me.

"Ah. You have feelings for this girl then?" I hoped my face didn't show any emotion. *Act like she doesn't matter. Do it, Gabe.*

"I don't want her to get in my way." I said finally, rolling my eyes for emphasis.

After a long while, he spoke. "Fine. We don't need her anyways. We need you. I need to know that you'll be behind the scenes." He gave me a knowing look, but I felt lost.

"Behind the scenes?" I sounded the words out carefully. *What was happening? This wasn't a part of the plan.*

"Well, Jared will go after Lena, of course. He won't let her go that easily. It is obvious if what you have told me is true about what is between them. Is it true then? They think they are in love?" He seemed bored with the question.

"Yes. They are in love." I said simply, but the rage on his face was apparent.

"They don't know what love is. No one does. Love is a figment of our imaginations. Lulling us to sleep, willing us to live. It's all nonsense. They have known each other for all of what, three weeks? What do they think they're in? A sappy, teen love movie? Ridiculous." He scoffed under his breath. I didn't speak, and he shook his head.

"Anyways, the point of this is that I need you to speak to them now. All of them. All those who were sick and have the cure. Lead them. Show me you can be a leader to them." He said each word as if his life depended on the very sentence.

"How?" I said breathlessly.

"Simply by controlling them. I need something invented from you. I need something that will keep them under control forever. They will have a master. That person is me, but after me." He hesitated. He approached me, and put a hand on my shoulder as if he were my father. He held Lena with one hand with ease, while I could barely hold her up with two. "I will die, and I need them to have a leader when I am gone. It has to be you."

"How can I do that?" My voice came out hoarse. My throat felt like it was closing up at the thought.

"It's simple. Give up everything. Give your humanity to me." I felt like I couldn't breathe, and I gulped loudly. He frowned at the sound.

"You don't want to do this? You don't want to rule the world any longer? Are you afraid?" His voice was rising with each question. I couldn't think. I couldn't answer. Before I could stop him, he took his free hand off my shoulder, and backhanded me. I was in astonishment. I was just bitch slapped, and I was fuming.

"I'm not afraid. I'm especially not afraid of you, you wicked old man." I shouted. My face was inches away from his. He smiled.

"I was waiting for your anger. I knew it was within you somewhere. Get angry. Be angry at the world for the hate it created in you; the wickedness that's buried deep inside of you." He was smiling. I felt chills. He meant every word he preached. Every line he spoke was a sermon for his hate of this world. He was off his rocker.

"Back to what I was saying. They need a new leader." He paused. "Here is the truth that no one really knows. I want them dead. I want them hopeless. I want them to never feel safe again. They don't deserve it. None of them do. They don't realize it yet, but I am their savior. I am saving them from harming themselves any longer. Things that don't matter rule them all. Now I will lead them. I want someone to discover a true cure." I gasped at that.

He laughed at the appalled face I was making. "I do. I want them to believe someone discovering the true cure to the Black Sickness can save them. Then I want it to be ripped away from them by me. No true cure. No way to escape. I want them all dead."

I was puzzled by his words. "Then we would have no one to lead."

"I don't want anyone to lead. Not really." He waved his hand dismissively while turning his back on me. The conversation was over. I was at a loss for words. What was the point of this, if we would all be dead?

"Do you think you can manage to invent a control system like that?" He asked, interrupting my thoughts. I hesitated, and he took that as not answering. "If you're thinking, what's in it for you? Remember this." he paused and turned away from me. "I can control you. With her."

He didn't have to tell me whom he was referring to. I could almost feel the chills running down my spine as I imagined Holland's lifeless body in my incompetent hands.

Corruption

Chapter One: Won't Give Up
Jared

"YOU HAVE TO try harder." She cried out to me. I gritted my teeth, while furrowing my brows. My breath was ragged and tight. I felt as if my chest would explode, revealing my heart was no longer there, but instead a chest of stone. I couldn't feel anything without her near.

"Jared. It is like you aren't even trying." She shouted in between grunts once again. I felt my frustration rising, so I let go of the rope and sent her flying. She plopped down hard on her ass in the sand. I wanted to apologize but I just couldn't. I was angry just like she was.

She shoved the sand off her legs, and stood fast. I knew she was pissed by the way her eyes were burning into mine. She pulled strawberry blonde

14

strands of hair behind her ear. My best friend, Holland, was getting sick of me. It had been a matter of thirteen hours, and she was already sick of me. We were working on gadgets to save the girl I loved. We were the last hope, or so it seemed.

Did I mention the girl I love, Lena, is under mind control and has red eyes? She's also a robot. Oh yeah, my best friend, Gabe completely betrayed me and killed my girlfriend in front of me. Snapped her neck with a twist of the wrist. Your average, ordinary teen romance, am I right?

"Look. If you aren't going to help me, go sit your ass over there." She pointed me off towards the trees, and I scowled.

"You know, we both have had losses in the past thirteen hours. You think you could keep your dramatics to a minimum." I pointed out. She smirked to me while pointing to the rotting all around her arm as a way to show me who had it worst. When I said nothing, she pointed to her cheek, the worst of the rot, and I rolled my eyes, not because I didn't pity her, but because she was using it as an excuse to be a jerk.

"Oh Jesus. Are you going to use that to your advantage every time I don't work up to par for you." Her face fell, and I could see tears were going to be shed by the way she held her mouth. I huffed. *Way to go, asshole. Who is the jerk now?* "I am sorry. That was insensitive of me." I looked down ashamed at myself. "I am sorry." I said once more when she didn't respond, and I was afraid to meet her eyes. "I'm," A large object flying towards my head cut me off.

I ducked but it was too late. *Wack.* A battery the size of a baseball hit me square on. Well that would leave a nice bruise. "Okay, okay. Damn. I get it." I scowled. "And ouch." I said rubbing my forehead. She turned her head from me and continued to pull. I sat down and watched her from afar. I looked at her face and took a deep inhale at the sight of her. I had already watched someone else die from the disease. The disease that destroyed my life more times than I cared to admit.

This disease was manmade by my girlfriend's father, Dr. Alona. He made the disease for the good of all human beings. He wanted to find the cure for cancers, diseases and sickness. He was the good guy. Instead, my own father, Dr. Ravana, destroyed this by spreading the disease to all sick patients in hospitals. That was where the cure comes in. The cure was a chip that went inside the bodies of the infected. When the chip found its way inside, it spread through the body, creating an easy way to leave the mind fragile and the body weak. Easy way for someone to swoop in and use mind control. As it turned out, my best friend was the mastermind behind this cure.

I should have known. My father was a doctor. He wasn't a scientist like Dr. Alona was, and like Gabe was. It should have hit me that someone else was working for my father to create the cure. There was no way that he could create something so powerful.

"Jared?" Holland's voice broke me from my spell of thoughts. "Will you help me? I can't do it alone." She spoke the last part softly. I smiled to her and got up.

I took two steps before she started talking again. "Now I see how Lena must have felt." I felt my heart sink. Lena. I thought of her always, but there wasn't much I could do to save her right now. Lena was given the disease and eventually the cure that caused her to be completely a mindless robot.

Somehow I knew she would be dead soon, and the thought alone made me miserable. She was under Gabe's mind control, and I didn't see how there would be any coming back from that. All I wanted to do was save her from the world, but the world wouldn't stop until it had claimed her. It had already done so. She was gone from me.

17

When the time would come, I knew I would have to be the one to finish the job. I would tell her how much I loved her, and how much I still wanted to be with her. Then I would kill my father, and then I would have to kill Lena. This seemed inevitable now.

The silence we shared as we pulled was nerve wrecking for me. Normally silence filled me with calmness but right at this moment, my thoughts wouldn't shut up. I couldn't help but think of what I would have to do. Holland made a long sigh, and I jumped slightly from the sound.

I took a deep breath to prepare to hear my own voice again. "Do you realize that Lena is probably really gone now?" From the corner of my eye, I saw Holland peer up, but I kept my eyes locked on the task at hand. "But I don't want to believe that, I actually refuse to face that fact. She has to be in there somehow." I continued. She shook her head and I acted as if I didn't see it. I felt my throat getting tight.

"Gabe betrayed us, Jared and he controls her completely now." She paused and I knew what was next. "He snapped. He truly snapped." I pulled the rope with one wretched tug, and it finally was tight. I let go of the rope, and Holland was left gaping at me. Without warning, I pulled her close to me. Holland dropped the rope in an instant.

"He killed her, Holland. I was there. I saw it too." She moved her face away from mine. I moved it back to me while cupping her chin. I waited for her to look me in the eyes before speaking. "What the hell happened with him? You were with him the entire time. What did he do to get away from you and do all this damage?" I said through gritted teeth.

All she did was stare at me, causing my anger to escalate. "I want to know how he got past you unless you were working with him too." I shouted louder, feeling my grip tighten on her chin. I knew my anger should have been present ages ago but I was too upset to see logically until now. Now I was angry, my anger was being lashed out to her. I couldn't help it. I couldn't stop it. I wanted the truth.

I loosened my grip quickly when Holland began to cough. Tears ran down her face, and she hunched over in pain. I was immediately transferred in time to when Lena was sick with the disease as well. I let go of her and moved two paces behind.

"I'm sorry Holland. You don't deserve this." Holland had been given the disease as a payback to me or to Gabe, I didn't know which of us it was towards. Either way, it was horrible for us. But then again, Gabe was clearly gone and not on our side. As it turned out, he never was.

"There is no way that he is bad." She gasped for air, snot dripping out of her nose. I had never seen her this way. She was always put together, and confident. She quickly covered her nose with her hands. She looked up in embarrassment and I turned away to give her privacy. After a moment, she began speaking once more.

"There is no way I missed anything. How could I have? We were literally together every night and day." She froze for a second as if she were deep in thought. "Actually, I woke up almost every morning and he was gone." I quickly turned back to see her presentable once more.

"Aha!" I snapped my fingers and pointed to her. Instead of agreeing, she threw up a hand and ignored me before continuing.

"He did enough damage in a tiny amount of time. It's insane because I was with him always and he acted normal. Well, normal for Gabe." I nodded in agreement with a shrug. Gabe was a character. That was for sure.

"I parted from him for only three days. It was when we separated to meet up here. I left the safe house two days ahead of him, meeting up with the crazy Earth Saviors as a false new member, and Gabe left to meet up with you eventually at the compound.

We wanted to make a bigger impact because he would get in and hack the system, and I would help Lena, as I did help her escape back there." She stopped. "I mean, really, I saved her ass." I shivered at the memory. Lena almost getting shot in the head by her former best friend, Kaley.

"I was wondering how you got to be with Kaley and the Earth Saviors. You know, I was with Lena the whole time. She was searching for me. She said I was her target. What does that mean?" I finally asked. The question had been burning in me for so long, and I hadn't been able to ask anyone about it.

"They are given targets that they have capture or find. Their job is to kill, infect or bring to their leaders to be a part of their army." Holland explained.

"What is the point of all this, Holland? I don't get it."

"Neither do I, but I believe that there is something very big going on and we might be missing the catch of it all somehow."

"Well, we need a plan to get back in there." I said and watched as Holland shivered.

"Are you crazy?" she shouted. "I am not going back there. What would be the point?"

"You're just afraid." I said in a matter of fact way. She simply stared back at me as if it were the dumbest thing I had ever said.

"Yes the hell I am, as you should be too. They are going to kill you. Perhaps you missed it, but they hate you. They want you dead. You would be walking to your death."

"I know but I cant give up on the girl I love either."

"She is already gone." she screamed to me. Rage was all over her face. "Why are you chasing the dead? Why are you trying to be a hero? There is no world to be the hero of anymore. It's gone. We're gone." she screamed. I shook all over to the truth of it, but I couldn't give up.

"The world still rests on our shoulders. I'm not giving up, and neither should you. We are the only people who know the most about what is going on. You have to do this. *We* have to do this. Who does it for them? Who does it for the people who don't understand what is happening?" My questions seemed to soften her exterior but I was wrong in thinking so by the next words she said.

"What about Lena's robot hater friends? The Earth Saviors. Let them save the world. I know we didn't kill every single one of them. Remember Kaley escaped. She escaped because Lena was too weak to kill her. That's your Lena. Fucking precious, useless and weak. She had a kind bone, and in turn, she couldn't even kill the villains of this story. Damn it Jared. She is gone, why keep trying?"

I forced my anger down. "I'll ignore all the shitty things you just said about Lena and just remind you of what we all know is true." She looked down, avoiding my eyes, she knew what I would say next. "She is still the key to survival. Did you forget that?" I said as forcefully as I could.

"Wait. What did you say?" she said while peeking up.

I ignored her. "Look, we need a plan. What should we do?" I said to her. She looked glazed over for a second before shaking her head as if something was impossible.

"Well, I guess we will have to go in as one of them." She paused and I let her think. There was no way in hell they could believe we were on of them. Hello, glowing red eyes were missing. "Wait, I have a better idea." She began pacing back and forth. I followed after her.

"I could become a target again. And we both know you are already one. You're still the number one target. Everyone hates you. Like really. They all hate you." I rolled my eyes at that. "If we're targets, away from water, those mindless creatures will bring us back in. They will capture us. Or so they think so."

"What do you suggest as our plan?" I asked.

"You aren't going to like it." She said with an almost sinister grin. She laughed but that cackle soon turned into coughs. I cringed at the wet sounds coming from her chest.

As the coughs died down, she removed her hand from her mouth to reveal blood. I ran over to her but she waved me away. "We have to move and fast." She was in super mode as soon as she finished the sentence. She was holding up the knife from her bag.

"You are going to go back to the compound. Only this time, you will already be dead. Or so they will think." She said while holding the knife ominously in her hand. It sounded menacing, but by the looks of it, I wasn't the only one who would be dead soon. The blood coating her hand proved it.

Chapter Two: Is There No Better Way?

THE PLAN THAT Holland created was great, except I would be covered in blood. Not only my blood, but also Holland's blood too. The point was to get as much blood on me as possible. Holland was already bleeding, so she just smeared some blood on me.

I knew the disease wasn't contracted from bodily fluids, but still, I was grossed out. We made small cuts on my arms to create a blood flow. I felt weaker by the minute, but Holland convinced me that this was the best for both of us.

Then she broke my thoughts. "I think the disease is airborne now." I looked over in shock. *Shit. Okay, sure, just cover me in your diseased blood.* Okay, that was mean but I couldn't contain my thoughts. *Stay calm.* I tried to convince myself.

"I know I was injected with it. But the world. The world seems different." she shook her head slowly as she looked around. "For instance, this beach. Look a little funny to you?" I followed her gaze. The sand had pieces of tarnished body parts. Arms, legs, pieces of skin. The world was in disorder. There was no denying it. The sand had turned red from so much blood. It didn't stop there. Blood coated the island.

"It does look pretty gruesome down here. It looks as if there have been bloody battles along this island. Do you really think it is airborne? Where is the proof other than just looking at the sand?"

She hesitated. "Gabe and I warned everyone on the news to stay away from hospitals. If they listened, then how did so many people catch the disease? It has to be spread through the air now, right?" she was deep in thought.

"I don't have the answer. I wish I had all the answers, but I just don't." I told her sadly. I wished there was a way to make it all right.

Holland and I continued with our plans, and just added to the bloody mess. The sand was thrown on my body as well, to make it look as if I had been bleeding into the sand around me. I had to look as convincing as possible.

Holland began talking once more through the silence we had just shared. "When I had reached the Earth Saviors, as they called themselves, I had passed through many towns. All of those towns were destroyed. Bodies everywhere. The grass was no longer green. Hell, are the skies even blue anymore, Jared? Or is the sky tarnished with blood too? The world we used to know is gone. The love that held people together has been destroyed. I know that love didn't do this to our world. Hate did this to our world. And how can we go on as people with hate all around us? Destruction. Corruption. It never ends, does it?" I held her gaze as she continued.

"Inside the Earth Saviors club, there was death everywhere. I was with them for four days. Just four. I saw more death in those four days than I had in my entire life. Not the deaths we see on the movies, or the dead we saw at funerals. I saw bodies being ripped apart. Screams of terror that haunt me day and night." I felt chills coursing through my body.

"The thing is, none of them left to go to the hospital, they had been warned, and many caught Dermadecatis just the same. The Earth Saviors would rather have rotted their entire bodies. They would rather look almost like a zombie. Flesh eaten away, dried blood along their face and smell as if they were already dead. They would have rather had their arms cut off, just to have it regrow in worse condition than before just to not be a robot. Just to not be mindless like Lena. Can you imagine?"

She paused for an answer but I didn't give her one. I couldn't. I couldn't imagine. I wouldn't want to be controlled, but I wouldn't want to rot from the inside, out either. She broke my thoughts. "So essentially I am answering my own question, it is airborne now. I don't know how I didn't get this disease sooner."

"Did the disease mutate somehow? That has to be the only way." She didn't answer me. "I can't believe it. How awful things got and so fast." She shook her head with me. We were both two souls who were lost. Destroyed without love, without an answer and without hope. The world was forgotten, and so were we.

"Let's move on with our plan. And fast." She said hastily. I thought that meant that she didn't want to discuss the matter any further, so I went straight back to work. We sat in silence but she finally broke it again. "If it is airborne, we will all be doomed." She didn't have to tell me twice. The truth was, we were already doomed.

"I know." I didn't want the disease but it would be inevitable. Why not speed up the process of getting the disease by getting cozy with a pile of infected blood?

I hoped Lena would be the one to retrieve me. If someone else came, I was afraid they would just kill me on the spot. Then again, my father probably wanted to take his precious time with my death. I didn't know if this plan was going to work because I was not the best actor, but I did know that Holland was. She would be the master of the show. She had many years of being dramatic in every situation that she should be able to fake anything.

"Do you think they will actually find us?" I asked. I was sitting in the sand. I kept throwing the bloodstained sand on my body to keep it fresh. Holland took out her compact mirror. She rose it to her eyes, and I watched as she took a deep inhale. She couldn't stand the way she looked now. I knew from the way her face darkened as soon as she saw herself. I knew from the gloom that fell over the air. I couldn't stand the sight of her either now; it just illuminated my latest failure. Her.

"First off, you will lay in the sand, far from the ocean and closer to the jungle part of the island. I want to say that when we move away from the water, there will be a swarm of people, including Gabe." She paused as she shivered with remembrance of what Gabe had done. I couldn't forget. I wouldn't let myself forget what he did while she probably could forgive him eventually. "The thing is, I don't know why Gabe couldn't come get us himself. Can he go near water?"

I paused. "Gabe is the controller, the master. He is not one of the controlled. So why wouldn't he go near water? I paused. "Maybe they're afraid of us then?"

She was cackling again, that wet sound coming from her chest just wouldn't stop, and it caused chills to go down my spine. "Don't make me laugh, Jared. No. You're the only thing that's threatening to them. But still, if there were ten against just us, that wouldn't be very menacing at all. Especially in my state." She sighed and turned her attention back to her reflection in the compact mirror. She grimaced.

"How do you even have that mirror?" I asked with suspicion. "Your priorities are super straight." I said with a smile.

"Hello. You think I don't walk around with makeup and mirrors twenty-four-seven?" She grinned at me and I couldn't help but let out a chuckle.

"What's next, chief?" I asked her. She frowned immediately as she attempted a smile. I knew it was because it hurt to smile. She was rotting faster than Lena ever did. The disease was advancing, mutating right before my very eyes.

They had more time to enhance the disease, and it killed me to know that the world was going under day-by-day, month by month. It seemed as though the moment that Lena was captured, the world had floundered.

"Holland?" I asked through the silence.

She turned to me with an evil glare. "Hush." She said, and I frowned as her focus shifted.

She wasn't watching me, but I pretend locked my lips, and threw the imaginary key in the air, and turned to the sea. The ocean. It reminded me of Lena. Lena loved the ocean. I remember the day I brought her to the safe house. She wanted to be near the ocean so badly. It warmed my heart when she did that.

The safe house. It reminded me of the life before the disease, and before things were hard. I didn't know where things went wrong with Gabe. We had been friends for as long as I could remember. And without a trace, without a serious motive, he switched teams. He was my best friend. The one I could count on, and now he was the one who wanted me dead the most. I left the safe house to find Lena and then everything went to hell. Holland was with him the entire time. How did she not see the truth?

I shook my head to myself and then froze as my thoughts ran wild. I couldn't help the thoughts that occurred, I couldn't help the feelings that were coming over me as I analyzed the situation. I knew the thoughts were wrong, and I shouldn't even flirt with the idea that Holland would betray me too, but it only seemed logical. If Gabe could do it, so could Holland. Holland wasn't with me, she couldn't be. She had to be on Gabe's side. Right?

She broke my thoughts, but the panic in me was still rising to the surface as it had earlier tonight. "So the plan. Let's go over it again, more thoroughly this time." She stood quickly. I simply nodded.

"Okay. I am going to hit you over the head. So it looks like there was a struggle. Then I will spill some more of my own blood on you. That way, it looks like you killed me." I grimaced at the thought. If Gabe knew me at all, and he did know me, he would know that I didn't kill her. I couldn't kill Holland. I couldn't betray my friends like he could. "Then, it will look like you are on the brink of death. I will hide here pretending to be dead, so I can breach the system from this island." *Right. What could possibly go wrong?*

I wanted to believe her but it was very hard at the moment. "Got the plan?" she said quickly, and I nodded. My thoughts were still running, but I had to let them go if this was going to work.

I got the plan. She would somehow betray me. Wouldn't she? "How do you know they will leave your "dead body" here?" I asked sarcastically. She looked at me full of anger, and I cringed away.

"If they take me, I will breach the system there while they deal with you." she paused, and examined my face for a moment. "I know you don't trust me." it was like she could hear my thoughts. She didn't elaborate any further, just extending my unease.

"Why do you say that?" I asked silently.

"Well, you think I am going to betray you as Gabe did. I won't though," she hesitated, she reached for my hand and I let her take hold. "We are in this together."

I nodded and embraced the warmth of her hand in mine. I had to think logically, she was the only friend I had left. I was all she had left too. I had to believe that she wasn't truly capable of betraying me. Although my head was finally agreeing that Holland was with me, I couldn't get the aching feeling in my chest away that she wasn't on my side. And we all know the heart is always right, don't we? I didn't trust her. I couldn't allow myself to trust blindly ever again.

Chapter Three: After Burn

WE WERE SITTING ducks waiting for all the details to look just right so that Gabe and the robots would believe we were both dead and gone. My fear was gaining speed as fast as the time was flying by.

I couldn't help it. I couldn't help but be discouraged that Holland would ever truly *not* be on Gabe's side. She loved the monster. I knew that Holland had stayed with me through it all, but I couldn't help where my mind wandered. In the safe house, she was great. She was there for me, she was there for Lena, but she loved Gabe. There was so much you would do for love. I would know.

I couldn't help the sting in the back of my mind reminding me not to fall victim to lies anymore. I had fallen prey to too many lies in my lifetime. I was too trusting, that was my weakness. And they both knew it. All too well.

The wind picked up around me, and I felt the burn in my eyes. Chills ran down my spine as I shivered against the cool air. Holland's face was turning redder by the minute as the wind whipped against her face. Her eyes were shut and her mouth was slightly agar. She was in pain. The temperature seemed to drop by many degrees in that moment, as night was finally upon us. I watched her face in the newfound darkness. Her eyes were still closed. I wondered what she was thinking.

"Holland, when should we make our move?" I said after the lingering silence. She peeked one eye open to look at me, before shutting it back.

"I know that Gabe is probably scheming as well. So I think we can wait it out for a few more hours and then we can make our move." I smiled because I had been counting on his schemes. All his schemes were always the same; get in, get the job done effectively and slowly. He wasn't exactly the master of speed.

Truthfully, my heart ached when I thought of my friend, my ex best friend. He was brilliant, he always was, and now his mind was being used for evil.

I knew all of Gabe's flaws, and in turn, he knew all of mine. He would count on my weaknesses, as I had counted on his. It was weird to be on the other side of Gabe. Enemy and not best friend. It felt so unnatural for me to hate him, but I did, and I had to defeat him. If I didn't defeat him, everything would be lost. The life I held dear, the lives I held dear, would all disappear from me into the dust.

"Well, I guess we can make a fire because it is a little chilly." She said through the dense air. *A little? I felt like the air was going to turn me into an icicle.*

"Should I go look for some wood?" I asked her when she made no move to start the fire. Instead, she looked as if she were chattering at the mouth. She had slightly crouched over, in an attempt to warm herself. My thoughts of our escape vanished in this moment. Even if I had fear of Holland being with Gabe, I knew that she needed warmth.

Her eyes popped open, "Sure. I can help." She rose slightly, and I could tell that she was winded because she stumbled to the left.

"No." I rushed to her side to push her gently back down on the log she sat on. "I will get it myself."

She smiled to me as she lowered herself back down. "Okay. Thank you." I rubbed her arm in response. I wished we had a blanket or I had a jacket to give her to wrap herself up, but we had nothing.

I walked through the wooded area behind us. I knew it wouldn't take long to find some wood. I knew trying to start a fire might take a little longer than it needed to take. I wished Gabe had created a way to make a fire start with just the mind.

As I stepped into the wooded area, I heard a shriek. I froze in shock because the sound was so eerie. I shouldn't have left her alone. I shouldn't have been out away from the water. It was too soon. The plan was ruined. I pivoted around to hear another scream.

From my view, I saw that Holland was no longer seated. I had to stop myself from being foolish and shouting her name, because I knew whoever took her would be waiting for me. They had to be.

I crouched down on the ground, and crawled until I knew the tree hid me. I peered out into the night for movement, but there was none. There was nothing to be seen in the night. Where was Holland? Did they just snatch her and leave? Did they kill her and I just didn't see yet. Were they waiting for me? Did they know I was hiding behind this tree?

These thoughts were rushing through my head, when I heard a snap behind me. I jumped a mile a minute at the sound. I turned quickly and relief washed all over me when I saw that it was Holland.

"Jesus. You scared me." I whispered harshly. She didn't answer, but instead continued her prance towards me. A chill ran down my spine as I watched her smile grow. She looked creepy as ever in the darkness, the moonlight seeming to illuminate the rot on her cheeks.

"Holland?" I asked quietly. She put a finger to her lips and pointed forward. I followed her finger to see three figures walking towards where Holland had been sitting once before.

I watched the hunching walk of one of them, and immediately recognized it was Gabe. Gabe turned towards the tree that Holland and I peeked around. I shook all over when his red eyes pierced the night. His eyes bore into the wooded area, and I prayed that I was not revealing much of myself. I slammed my back against the tree, and attempted to catch my breath. Holland was huddled down, still peering around. I wanted to tell her to make sure she was hidden, but I was afraid they would hear.

I tried to be as calm as possible as I peered back around. Gabe continued to look at us, or in the general direction of us. I couldn't look away this time. I couldn't be a sitting duck. I would have to attack and protect Holland and I. Finally Gabe lost interest, and turned away from us. I was able to breathe again.

I turned back around to Holland, but to my utter surprise and shock, she was gone. Now was time to panic, and panic I did. I started to hyperventilate silently, as my eyes searched the night. Where could she have gone? She was just right here. I looked back up to find Gabe, to see if Holland had joined his side.

The two men stood watch behind Gabe as he was now searching through our belongings. Bastard. But where had Holland gone?

That was when I felt something approach me, too close for comfort. The warmth of their breath touched my ears and made me shift away. I attempted to turn to face my intruder quickly, but rough hands forced my face forward instead.

"Trust me, Jared. Please." She said in a sickening voice. Before a second went by, I watched as Gabe and his two followers, lurched towards us in the woods with supersonic speed. They must have heard her voice; her awfully quiet voice in the night. I turned around to see Holland holding up a large rock. She had it raised over her head.

The pain was so strong as the first dig nailed me in the head. I fell to the ground with a clump, meeting the dirt face first. I felt a kick in the side, and I groaned as a mix of sand and dirt entered my mouth. Holland pushed me over so I was lying helpless on my side. All I could feel was betrayal as Gabe approached her smiling. He kissed her softly on the mouth, and she smiled deeply at him. My heart clenched. I was right then. Gabe turned his attention to me soon after. I felt sick.

"Surprise." He smiled intensely and leaned down to me. "Holland's with me." Gabe said as he took the rock from Holland's hands. "Well, this probably won't hurt as bad as it does to be alone. You tell me." He cackled into the air. It was the last thing I heard, that bitter, hateful sound, before he slammed the rock once more into my forehead. Everything went black.

Chapter Four: The Blurriness

ONE MISSISSIPPI. I was coming to. I could finally open my eyes. Only enough to shut them quickly again.

Two Mississippi. I can feel it. I can feel the beats of my heart pounding in my ears. The blood rushing in my veins. I can feel it.

Three Mississippi. The sound of muffled sounds erupted around me. They say things like, "we finally got him." *No, you don't have me. You don't have my soul just yet. My will. You don't have that either.*

Four Mississippi. I hear Lena screaming. I hear shouts, and then silence. She is being shut up quickly by her leader. Was she fighting? Was she fighting for me?

Five Mississippi. I realize that I have been betrayed. Twice. Hell, I've been betrayed endless times. Once by my father. Then my brother. Gabe.

Holland. As for the rest of the people who have betrayed me without my knowledge, that's to be continued.

Six Mississippi. I am being chained back up. I feel the slicing of the nails on the chains. I feel the bitter coldness of the metal. It makes my teeth chatter. It doesn't really matter though; nothing really matters at this point. I have given up. My body knows it, my mind knows it, and most of all, my heart knows it.

Seven Mississippi. I hear water dripping from a pipe. That water starts to run down my skin. It causes me pain for some reason. It causes me fear because it is warm water.

Eight Mississippi. I finally realize that it is my blood dripping to the floor, running down my body and splattering on the floor. As my eyes flutter open, I watch as the puddle begins growing. I will die here.

Nine Mississippi. I look up finally. My head barely holding itself up. My two best friends are standing before me with knives in their hands. They kiss slightly, and I see that Holland's eyes are not red. Yet.

No more Mississippis. I know that my time is almost up. And what did it really matter if it was up or not? At this moment and time, I knew that I was the only person in the entire world, who knew the truth and wanted to stop the madness. The sick injustice of a world where no one's mind was entirely their own anymore. I knew what to do but had no power behind me. I was only one man. Just as Sebastian Alona was only one man. He tried his best to create an antidote, and he couldn't do it. There was just so much you could do alone, when the entire world was working against you.

I was the last hope of the entire world, and I was strung up on two poles, with chains colliding together to hold a fragile, beaten down man. I was the man who couldn't be saved, who couldn't be anything but hopeless, full of loss. All hope was just that, lost.

My death was fast approaching me. I didn't want to die. I had too much to do, but as my blood splashed to the ground, it didn't seem like there was any other way. If I died, the truth died with me. No one would be left to defeat them.

"Kill me already." I spat to them. Holland winced at the sound of my voice. She faced me, with sadness on her face. I wanted to slap the look off her face, and I felt the anger boil in me. "Holland, don't act like you are hurt to see me this way. You can blame yourself when your pretty face rots away or when Gabe kills you because you're worthless to him.

Or he can control you. I bet he'd love that." I shouted in the dark, damp room. Holland flinched away and looked down, I just glared at her before forcing my head back down. It hit me then that I wasn't chained in my father's office like before. I was chained in a basement area.

Here I was trapped, again. The hero of the universe (if I could even be labeled as that), trapped for a second time over the course of two nights. I was betrayed twice, and let's face it, that was my hamartia; I trusted too easily. I let people in too fast. I let my love blind me from the people who wanted to see me hurt. If I had just opened my eyes, and ignored the fact that Holland had been in my life for years, I would have trusted my gut. I would have trusted my instinct that she wasn't with me.

That was when I felt him approaching, but I didn't bother to look up at him. "We will kill you when we are given the word. We're actually waiting on something you may be interested in knowing. But of course, you'll be dead soon so you're probably thinking, why should it matter to you? Let me tell you." He paused for dramatic effect but when I didn't so much as glance up at him, he continued.

"Well, Lena saw you beaten down and screamed when she saw you." *I was right. She was*

fighting for me when I was unconscious. It wasn't a dream.
"So that means, she is more challenging to control. We knew this, but I put the ultimate hold on her, and yet, she continues to fight me."

I could sense the frustration he felt in his tone. "Everyone else is responding quite well to the new technology I am using to control them. You see, when I snap their necks, I kill their human part, and they are reborn as full-blown robots. Lena didn't seem to respond, as she should have. Her humanity should be mine, and somehow it isn't." He began pacing. I could see his feet moving ahead of me.

"With all that being said, we have deemed her useless. She just gets in the way of operations. But first we want to run a test." This forced me to look up. I met his red eyes. "I made a few adjustments to Lena specifically. I want to see if she will lose it even after those adjustments have been made. We are going to kill her but first, she gets to watch you die."

I lifted my head finally in anger. I wanted to burn his face of with my stare but I didn't have the power. "We want to see if you dying would affect her again. See, her scream lasted for a second and that means she got control for no time at all. So that is much better than her getting, say, five minutes of control. What can you do with a few seconds? Not much." He smiled his sick little smile. I made no face back at him. I kept my face blank. He cleared his throat. He didn't seem to like it when I didn't respond to his evil plans. "Anyways, if Lena doesn't react, then she gets to keep her life."

"What life?" I asked. "This isn't life. For anyone. Even you. Aren't you tired of hurting people? Aren't you tired of making people your puppets?"

"I've never been so happy, Jared." He said simply. I tried not to be phased by that. "People finally answer to me. I am finally the most important person in the room. I am the most important person in thousands of lives. I control everything." He smiled. It was a creepy smile and I tried not to cringe away from it. I felt lightheaded, but I wouldn't break eye contact with him.

At least Lena and I would die the same night. Lena was the last hope for a cure, and she would be dead. I was the last hope to stop this all once and for all, and I would be dead too. I had one job on this earth, and it was to figure out the antidote that Dr. Alona had left for the world, and protect and care for Lena. I had failed on both accounts.

"We will leave you to your thoughts then. My lady and I have business to uphold. First, I am going to get rid of the rot in her body, because I have that power." *He had a true cure for the disease?* I was at a loss for words. He had a true cure. This changed everything. "Then, I want to tell her how much I love her, and how happy I am that she joined my side. In such an unexpected way, at that. So if you will excuse us." He kept rambling on. I fought the urge to vomit from his sappiness. They didn't share love. Neither of them knew what true love meant because they could so easily betray their friend. Holland smiled deeply and kissed his cheek.

As Gabe turned his back, Holland looked back at me, and winked as fast as she could. It was so quick that I wasn't sure if she meant to do it until she threw up her hand behind her back in the symbol that she and I had learned together at the age of ten; the trust symbol.

I blinked fast; I wanted to call out to her. What was happening? Gabe turned back to me, his red eyes boring into mine, and before I had time to think anymore. I was under. My brain felt like mush, and I was out before I could even comprehend it.

Chapter Five: The Pact

AND I WAS floating. I felt like I was floating through the air. All in all, I was completely lost. There was nothing that made sense to me any longer. The only things that filled my mind and heart lately, was confusion, hopelessness and despair. To complete it all, I didn't know what side Holland was actually on. What game was she playing? And whose team did she play for?

When Holland and I were in elementary school. We made a pact. It was a great pact. It was a childish pact. One that Gabe wasn't included on, and that was how we liked it back then. We didn't trust him well enough at the time. We filled our days with laughter, throwing the sign up behind Gabe's back all the time. It was a silly memory, one I hadn't ever forgotten though.

"Shake my hand." Holland said in a small voice.

"Why?" I said uneasily.

"We have to know that we won't tell anyone our secret!" she smiled her wicked smile. "Come on. We didn't include Gabe. He would be just heartbroken if he knew we did this without him!" I shifted uneasily. It didn't feel right to not share something with Gabe.

Holland smiled and batted her eyes to the best of her ability. "Is that your attempt at flirting? Because it is bloody awful." I said loudly before she shushed me.

"Give up that fake British accent. You suck at it," she laughed at me and I rolled my eyes at her. A moment passed before she spoke again. "Well?" she said cautiously. She knew not to continue her taunting game because she didn't want to risk losing me in our deal.

"Fine." I extended my hand to meet hers, but it ached with the truth that I was ultimately betraying Gabe. He liked Holland. I knew he did, and I couldn't believe what I would do.

"Now. Come on." She smiled again. "This is practice. We both wanted this to happen so we could be experienced when the person we liked actually came along." She was blushing now, and I felt the warmth reaching my cheeks as well. I nodded.

She leaned in as close as she could, and I closed almost all of the distance. It didn't feel like anything but how it felt when we were about to hug, until she leaned in more. She kissed me softly on the lips, and I waited for the hurricane to engulf over me. But nothing happened.

She jerked away and stared at me. "I feel." She paused, my heart started racing and I inhaled deeply. Please tell me you felt nothing too. Oh god, what have I done? "Absolutely nothing." I released my breath. Thank goodness. It's not that Holland wasn't beautiful, but her friendship meant more than anything to me. "What is all that nonsense about fireworks?" she gaped at me stupidly.

"Holland, the general idea of kissing is to do it with someone you actually like." She looked down to the ground. The blushing was starting again, but she nodded in agreement. "Cheer up. Don't you go acting different on me, mate." I tried my lousy British accent again, and that got her giggling but her gaze was still down. I tapped her shoulder until she looked at me again. "At least, we won't be nervous when the real thing comes along, right?"

"Right. You're right." She said while she grinned up at me. I smiled back.

"Holland. Come on. I am sure Gabe is searching for us." I said.

I turned my back and started to walk across the playground, blushing because I was sure someone had seen us. Or knew what we were up to at the very least. What if Gabe found out?

My thoughts were interrupted when Holland run up beside me. "I am glad that my first kiss was with you, Jared." She smiled to me and I felt myself worrying a little but she intruded my thoughts quickly. "We are just friends. I think I really like someone else. I just don't know yet." Let me guess, it's Gabe. I wanted to say but decided against it. "You're the best friend for doing this. Now we both have our experience. Here we need to make a symbol, a pact of some sort."

"Like what? A code word? Gabe will be suspicious of us." I said.

"No. Something with our hands."

"Like a gang symbol?" I giggled furiously as Holland just gaped at me.

"Fine. No symbol. No pact." She turned grumpily and I reached for her back.

"No. I love it. It's our secret. Our inside joke. Come on. What is the symbol?" I encouraged her.

"Here is to our pact." She smiled brightly as she turned away from me. As she did this, she brought up both hands in a crossing motion behind her back. Both fingers were crossed and I smiled brightly as she did this.

"This can be our way of knowing we're best friends. Always best friends. Us against Gabe, if you will." She nodded to me to tell me to do it back. I did it the best I could

as she giggled loudly. "You look silly doing it. I would practice." I scowled.

"You look pretty dang silly too, but I would never say that out loud." I shouted.

"You just did! Last one to the swings is a rotten potato." She screamed, as she scurried away from me.

I ran after her but as I took my first step, I saw none other than Gabe, watching from afar, a cold look on his face that brought shivers down my spine. He knew. His face told it all.

Yes, the memory was childish; the symbol was childish as well, but it didn't matter. The pact stood for years. Although we had stopped doing the symbol after the age of fourteen, it meant something to us. The symbol of our very friendship was used before my eyes just after she betrayed me for the first time in my life. It meant she was with me; it had to.

Chapter Six: "I'm Sorry" Just Isn't the Magic Word Today

"GOOD. YOU'RE AWAKE." Holland spoke loudly in my ear. I glanced up to see her right in front of my nose. I jerked my face away.

"Get. Away. From. Me." was all I could get out. Just like that, in between breaths.

"Look. I am here to tell you that Lena is still looking for a way to get out of our control but she won't try when you're dead. She won't have a need to try anymore." She smiled at me, and finally moved from my face. I could see behind her. Gabe was staring his dark, red eyes at me. It was like he was taunting me, silently. Words weren't needed to see the hatred he felt for me.

"Gabe and I want to talk to you about what really happened; what exactly happened your whole life." I didn't respond, and Holland laughed. "No fight left, dear?" I didn't answer again, and silence filled the air.

"So I was thinking we could tell you together." Gabe spoke through the bitter quiet. My head was hung low. It felt so hard to be awake. I longed for the memory of Holland and I when we were kids, just to fall under once more. I felt as if the air from my lungs would give up at any moment. I had so little fight left. My energy was scarce but I wanted to look at them. So I took what I had left and looked them in the eyes.

"We were your friends. We really were your friends, but then we were promised money, control and power. Who could turn down the money and glory? We had to decide what was more important. And what is more important in this world? I can assure you it isn't friendship and love."

The way he spoke was sinister, and I shivered ever so slightly. Gabe's words would have cut deep if I didn't expect them already. "We just were given the opportunity to make a difference. The world was falling apart, so do you fall with it or do you create the fall?" He was throwing his hands dramatically around to make his point. "We chose our side, and you chose yours, Jared."

"I unwisely thought you chose my side. You lied to me." I said.

"It's not about lies anymore. Don't be foolish." He scoffed. " It's about the simple fact that the world is dying. The world was dying before the spread of this disease anyways. Dr. Ravana taught me that. I didn't want to die. I wanted to be invincible. I wanted people to turn to me." Gabe was shouting now. He was very emotional about his truth.

Holland touched his shoulder to calm him before she stepped forward to face me. "Jared, when you left for the square, we really hoped you would die. We were planning a betrayal that neither of us wanted to do. We were just going to turn you in to your father, but then Lena happened. We didn't know that you would fall in love. We didn't know that she would fall in love in return. She stayed locked away in that house, just rotting away." Her face turned into a smile. "No pun intended. Your love." She sighed. "That was a plan neither of us could have planned. We had a weapon against you. Lena."

Gabe stepped in. "I created the cure for your father while you were living with me. I was right under your nose betraying you." He smiled at the exquisite pain he thought it caused me. It didn't. Not anymore. "You could have always been on your father's side, but you wanted to be good. You acted like you owed the world something, when the world should have been paying its dues to you. You just chose the wrong side. That is all."

Holland took over again. "We put a tracker on you. It is in your leg actually. Gabe made a silent, painless injection while you slept one night. That's how we knew where you were at all times. You made all those stops, the hospital, and the motel. We saw it all. When we knew you were in route, we followed on our screen. I was at the hospital, injecting all my patients with an immune system booster, also known as the disease."

My eyes widened in shock. Holland was a part of the nurses who were injecting humans with Dermadecatis. Even if she had thrown the symbol at me, she was a part of the problem. She did an injustice to the world. She was a part of the spread of this disease. Were they ever my friends? I didn't know but I would kill them if it were the last thing I did. I had a feeling it would be the last thing I ever did.

* * *

Holland stood there staring at me. Her face was twisted. There were mixed emotions she was running through, but I couldn't tell what was going on in her head. Gabe grabbed her by the hips and whispered in her ear. She smiled at him and kissed him once on the lips before leaving.

Whens she was gone, he stared at me with those red eyes before taking a deep breath. "Holland knew the plan." He sighed, and it felt like one of our normal conversations except this time I was chained up and he was my enemy.

"She knew that when you were at your weakest point, that she could rejoin me." He hesitated. He was rambling, something he did when he was unsure. "She did inject those humans with the disease." He stopped again and I rolled my eyes in response.

"Yeah. She just said that, Gabe." I say his name as if it were vinegar in my mouth.

He looked menacingly at me. "She did inject those people," he repeated, "Holland is a nurse. She loves helping people. I told her to go to the hospital to catch up with you. When she got there, there were nurses there. They told her to help everyone by injecting them with the cure to the disease. She believed it intensified their immune systems. She didn't know what she was injecting people with." *What?* "Hell, she didn't know what she was doing. I did though." *Holland didn't know what she was truly doing?*

"I tricked her. It's so easy to trick her." He smiled at me without humor. "She is so good, no, she was so good. She wanted to help those monsters, those useless humans. She didn't want to hurt anyone." He stopped but kept my gaze. "Truthfully, she wanted you in on the schemes when she found out what was truly going on. She begged all the time. When you reached the safe house, she was angry with me. She was done. She wanted to leave. She caused so many problems. She killed innocents. But you see she didn't leave my side. She loves me."

"It began differently. Holland thought she was injecting people with cures for diseases, those immune system boosters. She didn't know she was injecting people with the disease. When she finally discovered the truth, she was angry at first, but as always I could convince her to change her mind. Then she told me that she wanted to rid the world of bad people. The disease was given to criminals, I told her." He laughed bitterly and I cringed away from the sound.

"She is so naïve. The truth is, I didn't want her in this. I wanted her to not have any part. I wanted her safe but there is nowhere that is safe anymore. You're either on the side were the abuse is, or you're the abuser."

"So she didn't betray me." I whispered to myself. He looked at me like I was a pathetic man, which I probably looked pathetic at this moment, being chained up and all.

"She did betray you. Back to my story, before your rudely interrupted me." He scoffed before continuing. A scoff on him looked silly as ever with the creepy red eyes. Looked scary, but still the same weak man. "All along, she has said that she loved me and she was coming back for me. She understands what we are doing and trying to preserve. And now, she has joined my side finally, once and for all."

My heart was pounding. *What was she doing, really? This was the plan right? It had to be. She was fooling him. I had to believe that was what was going on here.*

He stared at me for another moment and scowled when I didn't say another word. He leaned back in his chair, throwing his hands behind his head and smiled. On the desk were about a dozen knives on a golden tray.

"Our next act is world domination. I think you will want to be alive to see it." I didn't answer as I had done all night, and he growled with anger. "Going to ignore me. Try to ignore this then." He picked the knife up from the desk.

He twirled it once menacingly, before chucking the blade right towards my heart.

Chapter Seven: Mirror, Mirror
Lena

BLOOD WAS POURING from my eyes as I stared at them through the glass. *Why was I bleeding? Was this some sort of dream?* The mirror. All I could think about was the dream I had where I chased a mirror. Could it have been this very mirror? Was it back to haunt me? I couldn't chase the mirror this time though. I stared at the haunting image of myself without blinking. I couldn't look away as the blood poured down my face, staining it red.

It was as if I were crying tears of salty blood, instead of salty water. Was it blood or was it just my eye tint now? Those red eyes glared back at me. I looked terrifying. I looked like a vampire crying. I couldn't speak, I couldn't move. I was trapped in my own body, in my own mind.

"Help." I wanted to shout, but there would be no sound. It would only come out in my mind. No one was here to help me anyways; not even me. I was a ghost beneath the control. Someone controlled everything about me. I was looking into that mirror with fierceness I didn't know I possessed. The image of myself was scaring me but I couldn't turn away. My body was stuck here.

There was an uncomfortable weight on me. It felt as if my lungs were collapsing, and my body would be immobile forever. I knew there was no one here pushing me down to the floor, I knew I was alone but I wasn't alone on the inside. Gabe was controlling me, and he was controlling me from a distance. He didn't have to be next to me. He didn't even have to look at me directly.

I could hear him. He was always in my thoughts, near me in my mind, taunting me. He was screaming to me, in my head. He shouted, "Stay put until I say differently. I want you to stare ahead. Stare at that mirror." And so I did, because nothing mattered but staring into that mirror. I stared into the emptiness. I stared into the void. It was hopeless. I was lost. My body was rigid, and I wasn't moving an inch because I wasn't myself any longer. I wasn't Lena. I was a number on his control range.

I felt like I had two minds inside my body. One mind was the Lena I love, the one talking right now. The second mind was this mindless being, which made me stay put. This was the mind that Gabe had complete control over. She was completely content with listening to a scared boy who used his intelligence to control her.

I wanted to scream. I wanted to rip open my body and shove her right on out, but I couldn't and she knew it, and if she could smile, she would smile because she knew there was no escape. There was no way out.

I was going insane, wasn't I? Where was Jared, and why couldn't he save me? I saw him being beaten, and taken. I felt myself coming through, but then Gabe grabbed control of me again. A part of me wished that Jared had given up, and left me here to live his life somewhere where they couldn't touch him.

What life?

The world was over. Even if Jared had given up on me, he would have to face a world alone. A broken, corrupt, vile world, where robots roam and evil geniuses rule. What kind of world is that?

If he got out of this alive, he would never be the same. The world had broken him with betrayal.

He had no one left. No one left who cared for him. No one who could show the love they felt for him. My love was trapped deep inside me, where the Lena he loved lived.

Jared was the love of my life, and I was his, but no one wanted to see something pure and good. No one wanted to see anything worthy of redemption. Instead, Gabe and Dr. Ravana wanted to destroy what was good in the world. They wrecked everything in their wake. They destroyed all that was decent in the world.

"Lena." Something whispered to me. I felt my skin crawling. *What was that?* I couldn't move myself, I couldn't move my eyes but before me in the mirror, I could see light around me, particularly around my neck.

What was happening? I panicked inside. I was swarming in a vast wonderland on the inside, but on the outside, my body wasn't moving at all. "Lena." It said again, and I was afraid, but it didn't matter. Someone could come up beside me and cut my throat, and I wouldn't be able to defend myself.

"This is the only hope. You are the only hope. Remember that?" I couldn't speak back but I knew that voice from miles away. I wasn't a voice that scared me. It was a voice I welcomed in my mind. It was my dad. He was calling to me, but from where?

The glowing was blinding, but I couldn't look away even if I wanted to. The sight enraptured me. It almost looked as if the light was coming from within me.

I wanted to touch it, to capture its very essence. Then, all of the sudden, the glowing stopped. My throat constricted. I felt empty without that glow, and I couldn't fathom why.

Before I had time to mourn the light disappearing, it sparked once more. I watched as the lights dimmed around my chest. Around the shocks of sparks, I saw my necklace. It lay on top of my breast. The necklace was more than just a key shaped necklace with diamonds. That key was the very spirit of me. My father, my mother, my family, my truth, my soul, all within a single necklace.

My father's voice once more filled my mind. "Listen to me carefully." And then he was talking at an inhuman speed, but I could keep up. Chills ran down my spine. He told me secrets. He told me he loved me. He told me exactly what to do. Just as soon as he was there, he was gone. As soon as his whispering stopped, the intense light went to a small glow, showing me that it was still working.

I felt my body in that moment. The trapped Lena was free. I was free. The ability to move seemed to return to me after he stopped talking. I could wiggle my fingers if I so choose to, but I knew I couldn't. I wanted to move, I urged myself to, but I still couldn't. I had to stay put.

Gabe must have felt the fight in me, because pressure was weighting down on my body once more. I felt Gabe there, but I felt myself over everything else. Gabe would never control me. He never truly could before, but now that power was gone from him forever as long as my necklace was around my neck. My father was here beyond the grave inside my necklace. He was here to wreck havoc on his partner's plans through me.

I had everything now. My secret weapon was with me the entire time.

Chapter Eight: The Secret

THE DOOR OPENED, and I forced my eyes forward to face that mirror once more. I couldn't move, and risk revealing my newfound power. "Lena?" Whoever it was spoke softly, and I squinted ever so slightly in the mirror to see who was behind me.

Clementine.

She scurried around, blocking the mirror and dropped on her knees with a thud in front of me, while gripping my face. "Oh shit. I am too late." She took a long look at my necklace. She always wanted it. I knew she would try to take it from me. I couldn't defend myself without giving myself away, so if she attempted to take my necklace, I would have two options. Let her, or kill her to hide the fact that I was no longer under control.

"It's glowing, that is good news." She was touching my necklace, a little too possessive for my liking. Then she tried. She tried to take it. As soon as her hand gripped the necklace, a breeze from an unseen force whipped my hair forward. The wind sped to a powerful force, and before I knew it, she was being propelled into the air. Without warning, she slammed into the wall the opposite side of me. She didn't move when she smacked head first into the floor.

Oh no.

"Shit." She cursed under her breath, and I felt like sighing in relief because she was okay. She picked herself up finally. She slowly paced back to me, before kneeling before me once more.

"Okay. I guess taking it isn't a good idea then." She laughed, but that laugh quickly silenced as she frowned. "This is extremely creepy. God, it's like I am talking to myself. Anyone in there?" She waved her hands in front of me but I knew I was staring at her blank, and red eyed.

"I didn't want to result to this, but I think this is the only way, isn't it?" I didn't answer. She knew I wouldn't. I didn't know why she was even talking out loud at this point.

She looked deep in thought, and she kept looking into my eyes. I faced forward, unseeing into her eyes, and didn't blink at all.

"Lena, this might hurt." On a normal day, I would have winced or throat punched her for whatever I thought was coming next. Instead, I waited for pain, but there was nothing. She stared at me for a good two minutes, and I wanted to laugh at how uncomfortable I was in this situation. I didn't feel a thing except a weird sensation running through my body. I felt like my body was being invaded in some type of way but I stayed still.

Finally, she broke eye contact with me. I wanted to exhale a big breath. I felt as if I were made of stone from the long encounter.

Her once black hair was brown. Her eyes were red before me and I felt fear that she had just revealed that she was evil too.

She stood suddenly and I wanted to gasp at the sight. Before me stood a woman with wavy brown locks, and red eyes. She was beautiful. Her stance was predatory, yet poised. She was me. Down to her red high heels. I couldn't breathe from the sight. *Did she just clone me?*

Then she spoke quickly. "Lena, I can now become you at any moment. You're probably afraid but don't be. If it comes down to it, they won't know who the real Lena is." She smiled at the thought, but all I could do was feel butterflies of nerves in the pit of my belly.

She sighed and rolled her eyes. "God, just like a wall." She shook her head as if to get the situation out of her head, and looked back down at me. "Lena, I am trying to help. You probably don't trust me or even like me, but I am a friend."

"I was a friend of Dr. Alona's. Truly I was. Please trust me." I felt my heart racing. She transformed back into herself in a blink of an eye. In that moment, I realized how much older Clementine was than me. It took watching her become me and then back to herself to see that simple fact.

"You have friends here. Don't forget who you are, Lena." She turned from me, and when she reached the door, she looked back at me with a smile. "I hope this isn't goodbye. But if it is, tell your family hello in heaven because that's where they will be, and that's where you will go. Tell your father I did everything I promised I would. Tell Jared how much he means to me too. Would you?"

She was gone in an instant, and all I could think about was what did she promise, and why did Jared matter to Clementine at all?

Chapter Nine: Straight to the Heart
Jared

THE KNIFE PLUNGED deep inside the mahogany wall, just an inch beside my head. I took a huge gulp of air. He missed me by an inch. Only an inch.

He stared at me with those red, angry eyes and he didn't look away. The silence was eerie as hell. I broke it quickly. "Why not just hit me with the knife?"

"That would be too easy, Jared. Don't you know that by now? We have had countless opportunities to kill you, and we let you walk away, alive, so many times."

"Why? What is the point of any of this?"

"You know the answer to that, Jared." Gabe rolled his eyes. I didn't, but I didn't ask anything else. He picked up another knife from the desk. "Let's play a game, shall we?" He teased me. I stared on uneasy.

"You tell me what I want to know, and each time you answer wrong, a knife will be thrown in your direction, how about that?" he smirked. He didn't give me time to answer before he asked something. "What did Dr. Alona leave for you in Lena's house?"

A note to keep Lena safe. That was my very first failure.

"No answer?" he screamed but I wouldn't budge. "Is that your final answer, Jared?" He raised his hand quickly, and before I knew it the blade was coming straight for me. The knife plunged into my forearm and I cried out in pain.

"That's just the first cut of the night. The easiest of the questions." He smiled at me and I wanted to knock it off his face.

He picked up the next knife, and twirled it around. "What is the antidote? Is it real? Does Lena have it?" The questions came out faster than I could comprehend. He didn't hesitate before throwing the knife at full speed towards my neck.

It punctured the wall. I could feel the cold knife against my neck, although it didn't knick me.

"I bet you're wondering why I am such a good thrower of knives, when I have never thrown a knife in my life." He rambled on. "Ask me why." He shouted.

When I didn't, he approached me fast and jerked my hair so I had to look at him. "I said, ask me why." He said through clenched teeth. He took the knife he had in his hand, and placed the cool blade on my forehead. I didn't speak. He pressed it into my forehead, until I felt the sting.

"Ask me."

"Why, Gabe?" I finally said as a small trail of blood ran down my face.

"It's funny you should ask." He said as he turned to walk back to the desk with knives. "I have all the powers of the robots now, but I am not a robot. To control them, you have to understand them. You have to know what they're thinking, at all times." He hesitated and stared at me for a long time.

"Here is the thing. I observe people. I have watched them for years, trying to understand why people were so rotten inside. I hated people. I loathed mankind for as long as I could remember. I wanted to destroy the way humanity was for so long. I wanted to change the hate, but I couldn't because I felt the anger. I felt the bitterness, and I couldn't change the world for good when I was so angry inside. I could only change the world for the worst. And now, here I stand."

"Your father hates humanity as much as I do. He taught me everything. Everything I feel, he felt first. That is why the two of us made such a good team. Lena's father created the disease for the good of mankind. He wanted to see the good in the world, but there is no good in the world. You're staring right at the pit of the world. I control it. You're staring at what hate and anger can do. Evil triumphs good every single time." I wanted to believe the contrary to that, but he was right. Evil was staring me right in the face, and I was the good one, tied up and unable to fight evil.

"Back to why I have powers that the robots have. I had to understand what I was asking them to do. I had to understand the power they felt, and I do. It is unlike anything I have ever experienced. I can look at you, and burn you to ash. I can fly through the night's sky without anything to help me. I have unnatural strength, energy. I don't need sleep, I don't need to breathe. I don't need anything, but I want. I want to control. I want to destroy. I want to ruin everything." His voice was rising with each moment.

"But the world will be gone soon. There won't be anyone left to turn into a mindless robot, and then what will you do?" I asked.

"I will rule."

"Won't that get boring?"

"To feel the power I feel. To feel that no one will ever disobey me. It is unlike anything I have ever felt. I had nothing before this. I have the world at my fingertips. I will never grow tired of pushing them down, after years of being pushed down by the world. Finally the world answers to me, and I don't answer to it."

"You said so yourself that the world was full of hate, all you did was add to it." I pointed out.

"Again, do you join the world in the fall, or do you create the fall? It's simple. You pick the winning side. Now enough of this." He took a new knife in his hands. "Next question."

"Are we really still on this? Are you just going to play, "Which knife will land in Jared's head?""

"Until I see fit for the game to stop, we will keep playing." He scowled. I rolled my eyes. "Why is Lena so hard to control? You must know. Dr. Alona probably told you why." I wanted to laugh at him. I didn't know anything, but he didn't have to know that.

"See Jared, I have been kind. I have purposely not hit you twice now. That will not last for long. I will hit you, until you are begging for mercy, or for death, and I will not give you either."

I just stared at him, as menacingly as I could muster in my predicament. He was fuming from my continued silence. His red eyes seemed to match his red face.

The knife came flying at me. There was nothing I could do to stop it from plunging into my skin. It pierced my hand as I howled in pain. I looked over to see the damage and almost retched at the sight. The knife handle was hanging out the front of my hand, while the blade was completely through the palm of my hand on the other side. Blood poured down and splashed onto the floor.

"Have you had enough of not answering? Or do you want to start giving me the answers that I so nicely asked of you?" He watched me with curious eyes. He approached me quickly, and jerked the knife out of my hand. There was both relief and pain from the loss of the knife. Blood was pouring, and I felt even dizzier than before. I didn't cry out this time. I wouldn't let him have the pleasure.

Gabe was right in my face, shouting more questions. "What does that necklace of hers mean?

Any time someone tries to take it, it reacts." I felt my eyes widening. *The necklace her father gave to her? The necklace reacts? How? That sounded ridiculous. How can a necklace have a mind of it's own?* I refused to say where she got it.

"I don't know what you mean by that. Lena has always had the necklace. There is no significance behind it." What if there was significance behind it? After all, her dad gave it to her, the day he died at that. The wheels were turning in my head. What could it mean?

"Are you lying to me, Jared?" Gabe asked suspiciously.

"Why would I lie?"

"Why wouldn't you lie to me, Jared? Why wouldn't you? To protect her, to protect yourself." He laughed humorlessly.

"How about I just take the necklace from her, and see what is in it?" Gabe said frantically. He was staring at me so intensely.

"You said yourself, it reacts if someone tries to take it from her."

"Hmm." He was thinking, and I let him. He snapped his fingers close to his ears. "Yes. Of course. I've got it." He pointed to me. "What if you tried to take it from her? She trusts you. The necklace won't react to you."

"She is under your control. She has nothing but callous feelings towards me." I said simply.

"You're right. This will go one of two ways. One, she will let you take the necklace, and that's good news for me. Second scenario, you try to take the necklace, and she kills you. Again, good news for me." He laughed his choked laugh.

"All I have to do now, is simply think of the robot I need. I shout to them through my mind, and then they come running to me. They listen to me, they would never betray me. They wouldn't dream of it." He was so sure of himself. He was so foolish. Lena had fought against his control so many times, and yet, he still thought she wouldn't betray him. When had he become so stupid?

"Those robots were once human, and humans turn on each other every chance they get." I stated his ideas back to him. He scowled at me. "Those humans that you hate so much are callous and evil, remember? They won't stand to be controlled forever." I knew it wasn't wise to warn him, but it felt so good to

"My technology won't let that happen." He was furious at my questioning of him.

"So science triumphs humanity? I don't think so." He was shaking at this point. I was mocking his religion. His life. His prophesy of the world.

"You won't be alive to see if that is true or not though. So don't worry about what will happen to me." Gabe said through gritted teeth. "Let's put it to the test, shall we? Let's see if she will disobey me ever again." He said cruelly.

This wouldn't end well for me at all. I held my breath before speaking. "Bring her in."

Chapter Ten: Whose Side Am I On Anyways?
Lena

THE DOOR OPENED and I saw him. The most beautiful man; he was here to save me. The devil was within him but I let him pick me up. I let him whisk me down the hall. I let him pull my body out of the skeleton that held me. Then I realized he didn't love the skeleton around me, and I got angry.

I jerked slightly. I had been daydreaming of Jared coming to save me. The truth was I didn't need to be saved. I could save my own self. I was alone. Jared was gone. He had to be. There was no reason for them to keep him alive any longer. As it dawned at me, that he could be gone forever, I felt the emptiness swim over me again. It felt like waves were crashing over me, repeatedly, but I couldn't die, I was just drowning. I was swallowing the water, feeling the pressure of my lungs failing me, but instead of the relief of death, I was imperishable, I couldn't be killed.

I wanted to get up and find him, but that would give me away. I had to keep staring into this mirror, choked inside at the unchangeable. The loss of Jared.

In an instant, my eyes began to glow. *The voices are back.* Although my mind was my own, I could hear them shouting to me. I had a new power. I had a new force behind me but their voices remained. There was one voice above the rest, Gabe. He screamed for me to get up and to come forward. So I did, and quickly. I was eager to see what he wanted from me now.

His voice went from a scream, to a whisper, and I knew he was gone from my mind. His job was done. He commanded me to come, and he knew I would come because I could only obey.

Or so he thought.

As I proceeded to walk away, I saw my necklace glowing brightly in the mirror. My eyes were glued to the mirror, captivated and yet, blinded by the glow.

"You decide whose side you are one Lena." A voice whispered to me. Father. It was father again. Whose side am I on? I knew whose side I was on. It was the side of humanity. Humanity. What an easy concept to blur. Humanity was innately good, but the people in it weren't.

I was on the other side of the wicked. It was on the side of the good people. I wasn't with Gabe. I wasn't evil. I was kind; I was good.

I smiled victoriously at myself in the mirror. My father was here with me always. I shook my head. I had been standing too long staring at myself. I knew I had to hurry before Gabe would be suspicious of where I was. I normally came to him without a moment's hesitation, but this was important. I had to listen to what my father wanted of me.

"Pick up the necklace, Lena." He said to me softly. I felt invincibility the moment it met my skin. It glowed into my palms. He spoke once more. "Open it now, and quickly. You won't be alone in your mind much longer. He is wondering where you are."

I tilted the key to the side. *Open it, but how?*

"Lift the first diamond on the key." I located the first diamond at the top of the key, and I lifted it with care. The glowing intensified further and he spoke once more, "I love you. The key has great power, and it only answers to you. The truth is within you. I cannot tell you more. Your mind is open to too many evildoers. Goodbye, Lena." It felt like these were his final words, and they probably were. I would never hear him again on earth.

The key opened further, and inside was a small red button. I pushed it. Nothing happened. *Oh no, it's broken.* I looked into the mirror and gasped out loud. My eyes were not burning red. They were hazel. *What was happening?*

In no time, I felt it. Something I didn't know I could ever feel again. A faint beating of blood entered my ears. I could hear it too. My heartbeat. I pushed my hand against my breast. There it was, a steady beat. I was human once more. But how?

I panicked for a moment. I was happy to feel human, but how was I to walk into the room and convince Gabe I was under his control. I pushed the button once more.

There it was. The button could reverse itself too. Red eyes. I pressed my palm to my chest again. Heartbeat was gone. I was a hybrid then. I wanted to giggle at the thought. I could turn from human to robot in seconds. All this power came from a necklace. A necklace I had worn for years before this moment.

I marched on as if I were a solider. I had to pretend to be, and play the part. To my surprise, I willed my eyes to see through the walls ahead of me, and I did. I could see within every closed door still. I still possessed my robotic powers. I would need them. I had to use them to my advantage. They weren't a curse to me anymore; they were a blessing in disguise.

My father must have known that I would need these powers still, until it was safe to become a human once more. If I could so easily turn back into a human, it meant that the others could too. Didn't it? I could change everything if I knew how to transfer my necklace's power to the world.

My father must have known what would happen to me, and what was to come. Did he want me to become a robot, to use these weapons against them? To defeat them? My father was a smart man, and this had to have been his plan. He was four steps ahead of Dr. Ravana and Gabe, when they thought my father was three paces behind.

As I searched through the walls, I knew what I was looking for. I quickened my pace, but not before grabbing a gun from the gunroom. I tucked it into my jeans. My shirt was big enough, that no one would ever see it. No one would suspect me to have a weapon because Gabe never told me to grab one. He only asked me to join him in the room down the hall.

I almost laughed when I heard Gabe barking another order to hurry. I could hear him, but he didn't control me. I moved at my own will. *Just let me get out of this alive.* I wanted to save the others. It was my duty to save the others now. I had the power now; I had the answers. I had the most important weapon. The antidote. I was the antidote.

Chapter Eleven: Got You, Count To Three

Jared

I FELT HER presence before I even looked up. The chill that ran down my back was still filled with so much love. I felt my heart quicken as soon as she entered the room. I met her eyes for the first time in what felt like forever. Although they were red, they had warmth. Her presence was the resolution of my being.

She was not a monster to me. She was Lena. She was the girl I loved, and for a moment, I forgot that she was under control. She didn't appear to be at all. That was the love I felt for her talking, and I was letting my guard down. I couldn't afford to do that, ever again.

Lena walked towards me as Gabe watched her every move with power hungry eyes. She was different but I didn't know how. She walked as stiff as ever. She used to walk as if she were on air. I couldn't understand, because her eyes were red, giving away that she wasn't the Lena I knew. Appearance wise, she looked under Gabe's control, but I couldn't get that nagging feeling out of me; that she was there somehow.

If I hadn't been watching her so intently, I would have missed it. Her eyes. There was a flutter in her eyes when she looked into mine. I felt my breath take in deeply. There was no way. It must have been a trick of the light because there was no way that this was true. Was she still in there?

When she reached me, I watched her ever so closely, willing her eyes to flutter again. She leaned forward and began to squeeze the blood from my arm. Pain shot through me, but I wouldn't scream. I wouldn't shout or thrash about in pain anymore. They wouldn't make me look weak anymore.

She looked me dead in the eyes, with almost a grimace. Before I knew it, she had lifted her hand high in the air, and slammed it quickly down on my head. Spots filled my vision.

I heard the snickers behind us from Gabe, and I felt my blood boiling. *Yup, she's gone. It was a trick of the light.* When I regained my eyesight, I saw Gabe and Holland laughing like they had heard the funniest joke. *When the hell did Holland get here?*

I spit out blood on the ground right by Lena's feet. "Shut the fuck up. The pair of you sounds like gagging hyenas." Gabe was beginning to turn red in the face at my words. He didn't even speak, but he didn't have to. Lena was ready for me. This time, she kicked me right in the stomach. I gasped for air, and if I could hunch over I would, but the chains held me up.

That was when her fist met my nose with a faint crunch. I would never look the same after all the times I had been beaten in this single night. That was appearance wise. The truth was, I would never be the same because I had lost so much.

"You know Jared. This is all self inflicted." Gabe finally spoke. "If you would just shut the hell up instead of telling us to shut the fuck up, then maybe this wouldn't be happening to you." He hesitated. "Learn from your mistakes." I was so over learning and failing, so I would make it my mission to ruin his ego instead.

"Gabe, oh Gabe." I laughed hysterically as if I had heard the greatest joke of all time. I was losing it. I wasn't in my right frame of mind to mock a man who hated me more than I hated myself. I had lost too much blood, which was the only way to explain it. "You are so weak. You only feel power when you're behind a robot. Be a man. Beat me yourself." His face was pure rage. "Oh wait. You won't beat me, because you know I would kick your ass in a fight. You wouldn't last two seconds." I wasn't finished speaking, but Lena cut me off with a slap to the face.

My cheek burned but I wasn't done. I would never be done. "You won't ever face off with me, will you? You've been afraid of me your whole life." He didn't answer but Holland was red in the face now.

"Jared, calm down." Holland yelled to me.

"Calm down? Calm down?" I shouted. "How can I calm down when my backstabbing, gagging hyena best friends have betrayed me?" Holland began to speak but I shouted over her, drowning out whatever she tried to say. "No, Holland. Shut up. You are the worst of them all. Gabe has always been a bitch from hell, but I didn't know you were one as well." I shouted. That was enough for Gabe.

Lena did a roundhouse kick. The crack against my head was insufferable, and I felt like my head was spinning in double time. My brain was feeling as if it had just been juggled around in my head.

"Fuck." I shouted. Lena moved from in front of me, and Gabe took her place. He took a grip full of my hair and jerked up, possibly drawing blood from my scalp.

"Have you had enough, Jared? Have you finally had enough?" Gabe shouted. He let go, and I let my head droop.

Lena was in front of me once more. I saw her shoes in my periphery, and I felt fear for the first time around her. She had beaten me to a pulp, and this was just the beginning. So when I saw her hand reach for me, I cringed away.

She reached over to where my hands were and caressed softly. The movement was quick and brisk. By some grace above, Lena rubbed her hand against mine and I felt warmth in my soul. I knew it was on purpose and deliberate because Gabe wouldn't want her to touch me affectionately. My heart quickened in response. She squeezed down lightly on my hands and I couldn't contain my smile. That was definitely on purpose.

She was hidden from Holland and Gabe. And I kept my head pulled down. As I continued to look, Lena slightly lifted her shirt. And as she did, I noticed a bulge on her right hip. I didn't know what it was until she made a signal with her hands as if she were holding a gun.

Lena had a gun.

"Come here, Lena." Holland barked to Lena. I jerked my head up quickly. Did they just see our exchange?

Gabe's red eyes bored into her. "I see you have disobeyed me." he said softly. And I listened with heightened ears, as my eyes closed.

"Give me the gun." There was silence, and I peeked my eyes open.

"Lena." He said as he reached his hand out to her. I held my breath. "Give me-" Before he could finish, Lena grabbed Holland and pushed the gun against her forehead. Lena didn't speak. She didn't have to.

Gabe threw his hands up in defeat. "Let her go." He said quickly.

Lena still didn't speak. It was as if she were struggling a little. "You know what?" He said with a malicious smile. "I don't care what you do." He put his hands back down, and turned away. Holland's face was pure betrayal, but Lena faltered in the slightest bit, but it was enough time. *Don't kill Lena, Holland. Please.* I pleaded internally.

Holland pushed Lena down while grabbing the gun from her hands. Holland turned the gun towards Gabe. He didn't even as much as turn around from the altercation.

"Holland." he said simply without looking at her.

Holland's grip loosened on the gun in defeat, but she gripped it once more after a split second. "You were going to let her kill me?" she said through gritted teeth. Her anger was terrifying to everyone but Gabe.

He seemed to freeze at that but relaxed quickly. He turned to face her. Red eyes blazing, cocky smile on.

"Baby, of course not. She loosened her grip on you, allowing you to get the gun. It was all a part of the plan. Now. Give me the gun." He said as sweetly as he could. I rolled my eyes as she handed him the gun. *Damn idiot.*

As they exchanged the gun, Lena finally popped up from the ground, ready to pounce on either one of them. Gabe kept his cool, and he wasn't afraid. He stayed in his slouched over state, not even erect from the dilemma. Gabe held out his hand, and Lena froze in mid stance.

"Now that this is over, you will shoot Jared." He said calmly to Lena.

He held the butt of the gun towards Lena, and she faced him as if she were a solider on command. Lena took the gun and turned to face me.

She lifted the gun fast. Her hand on the trigger. Her eyes red and fierce. She was gone. I could feel it. I shrank into my body. I guess it wouldn't be so bad to die by the hands of someone I loved.

Gabe had a frustrated look on his face and his brow was scrunched up in concentration. I watched Holland's hands twitching by his side in anticipation.

"Any last words?" Lena spoke in her magical voice. Her eyes bored into mine, completely lost. My love, my love was gone.

"I do. I love you. I love all of you in different ways. But one thing I don't love is the betrayal demonstrated by the two hyenas in the corner. You fucking deserve one another." I shouted towards them. Now Gabe was twitching with Holland now. Holland twitched with anticipation; he twitched with anger. They looked like two drug addicts, to be honest. I wanted to tell them, but I couldn't because Lena took one step closer to me. The gun was right against my forehead now.

I looked her deep in the eyes. "I love you, Lena." I said quickly. I wanted it to be my last words.

It all happened in slow motion. With one swift moment, Lena moved the gun from my head, and shot the lock on the chains on the ceiling, releasing me from the chains that held me up. I fell to the ground, scrapping my knees on the concrete.

One moment, the gun was facing my chains, and in the next second it was facing Holland. The shot was loud and left a ringing in my ears.

Holland went down, and then Lena's gun was facing Gabe. The third shot rang in my ears. Gabe fell sloppily to the ground.

"Let's give the gun to the girl you can barely control, geniuses." Lena shouted to them. "Let's go!" she screamed to me. She grabbed me from the ground and we took off, leaving the two of my greatest friends, yet greatest enemies on the ground.

Chapter Twelve: Escape
Lena

THE ADRENELINE IN my veins surged through my body, and forced me to move faster than I ever had before, even as a robot. I tugged at Jared's hand to get him to run my speed, forgetting that I had powers that he did not. This was it; we would finally be gone. We could make it if we kept going. I knew someone would try to stop us but I had a new power on my side. I had control of my own body, and I had my father to thank for that.

I knew I had taken control of myself on several occasions, but this time was different. My father had given me back my humanity. I felt like myself, but more powerful than ever.

"Jared. Try to keep up." I screamed to him.

"Let go of my hand. I think I can move faster without the pull." He said. He wasn't being rude or sarcastic, he was just stating the facts.

"Oh shit. Sorry." I said, letting go of his hand. He clenched and unclenched his hand to regain feeling in his hand. "I am sorry. I didn't think of that. I thought I was helping." I said as we kept running down the long, winding hallway. All the walls were the same, and it would be easy to lose our way if we didn't keep our minds open to pay attention to the details.

"Where is Joseph? Where is anyone?" I thought out loud. Jared didn't make a sound, so I looked over to him. Jared just shook his head.

"Didn't they hear the shots?" He asked. I ignored the question for the time being. I took the moment to use my powers.

I peered through each door as we ran. Empty. Every room. Where were the students? Theo? Joseph? Max? Aiden? This wasn't good. I didn't point this out to Jared. I didn't need to worry his mind any further. He looked terrible. He had been beaten down so many times tonight.

His nose was slightly crooked. His eyes were droopy. His face so swollen so much that he looked like a different man altogether. Dried up blood was caked all over his face. Jared was a handsome man, but I didn't know how handsome he would be after this night. It wouldn't matter if we couldn't get out of here anyways.

That was when I saw his hand. Thank god I hadn't been pulling that one. It looked damaged beyond repair. The hand appeared to have a hole in it, as if something had went clean through it. I wanted to stop right then and there, and turn around to destroy whoever did this to him, but it would just slow us down. I ignored it for now, but he knew I saw it. He watched me with knowing eyes.

"I have no idea." I finally said to his question. We kept on our way and Jared spoke again.

"Where can we go?" he said through gasps. He was getting tired. This wasn't going well. Where I felt energized and alive, Jared felt weak and apprehensive.

"We will figure it out. Stay calm." I knew he felt anything but calm though.

That was when he stood in front of me. Blocking us from escaping. I stopped suddenly, causing Jared to slam into my back. I gripped him to keep him steady. "Get out of the way." I screamed to the monster in front of me.

"How did you do it?" Dr. Ravana spoke silently. He looked like a frail old man.

"Do what?" I shouted impatiently. He simply stared at me, not answering. "I don't have time for this. Move, or I will kill you. I don't fear you any longer. Try and control me. You can't!" I screamed.

He smiled. A deep, serene smile. It wasn't malicious for once. I was stunned. Floored. He didn't have a genuine bone in his body. He looked deep in thought and he finally spoke. "Lena, look at you." He said affectionately.

I had enough then. He was done confusing me. He was done ruining my life, as he did to so many others. To the man beside me, to the people out there waiting to be saved.

I took my hands and made a swooshing motion to the side. Dr. Ravana went flying through the air, slamming against the wall. The crack was loud, and I wondered what part of his body he hit. He moaned in pain, but he deserved it. Blood began to spill from his head. Jared tugged me forward, but something held me back.

"Dr. Ravana?" I spoke silently. My humanity was my biggest flaw. I knew it. Jared knew it. And Dr. Ravana did too. "Dr. Ravana? Are you okay?" Jared sighed beside me in frustration.

"Lena. Come on." Jared urged me.

I was frozen. I couldn't leave him. I knew he was terrible. I knew he was the reason for everything but blood was pooling beside him from something I had done.

"Lena, what made you fight through the control?" Dr. Ravana asked through grunts of pain.

"Easy." I said almost as silently as he spoke. I reached down, but stopped myself before I touched him. "It was love." I said simply. He closed his eyes as if he were experiencing bliss. No one was around for miles, and I looked to Jared to see his confused face.

"I'm sorry I had to hurt you." I said simply. And he kept his eyes closed and I felt my body becoming weak with guilt. I couldn't feel it though. I couldn't feel remorse for him. He had never felt remorse for what he had done. He destroyed so many lives.

Jared tugged me once more, and I let him pull me away. We left Dr. Ravana to lie in his pool of blood on the floor.

"Love." He whispered into the dark. He was sighing as we ran down the hall. I had never been so confused in my life. Love saved me. Love could save a world even. Why was that so surprising to him?

PART TWO

Jared
Chapter Thirteen: Until the End

MY FATHER ALWAYS was a nutcase but now, now he was just plain weird. He didn't know what love was. He killed my mother. He killed my best friend. He tried to kill everyone I had ever loved. He destroyed everything that humanity held dear.

So you can understand my surprise when I felt a moment of heart for him. I felt a moment of pure forgiveness. My explanation? He tried to mind control me. And that's the only reason I found forgiveness in my heart for him in that moment.

That was it. That was why Lena felt that connection to ask him if he were okay. Otherwise, neither one of us would have cared. We would have let him die, right there. Isn't that the truth? Or was our humanity shinning through because we were good people?

I let it go. We were on a mission. A mission to escape. We continued running until we reached the door to the staircase. "Should we go down?" I asked quickly.

As we ran down the steps, we saw them. All of them. All the people that were absent when we had first escaped had suddenly appeared. They were crowding in front of us, Joseph their ringleader. And they were coming for one thing, us. They were running towards us on the stairwell at heightened speed. Lena and I turned quickly back and climbed our way back up to the top flight, taking two steps at a time.

When we reached the floor we were just on, we didn't stop there. We kept going up the flights of stairs. When we reached the top floor door, we went through it to find ourselves on the roof.

As soon as we shut the door to the roof behind us, Lena used her eyes to melt the handle, locking them inside, and us outside. We were definitely in the wrong direction. Our escape was meant to be through the basement, not the roof.

"Now what?" I shouted over the roar of the ocean. "What if this is it for us?" I knew the question was harsh, but it was a valid question.

She didn't meet my eyes. "This can't be the end." She said emotionally. I reached for her, and she let me hold her against my body.

"You're right. It can't be the end for us. I love you, Lena. We are going to be okay. We have each other. We can make it through anything." She turned to face me. She didn't have to say anything for me to feel the love.

She placed a hand on my cheek. "I love you too." I was just about to kiss her but she spoke once more. "We could-" She started, but her voice was drowned out by the sound of another.

"Well, well, well." His voice shouted over the sound of the ocean. There were so many voices that I had come to hate. I collected them. Their voices fueled my hate and pain. This voice being one of them.

Aiden.

"What do you want?" I groaned.

"I have many plans for the two of you, but first." He smirked at the two of us. I tightened my grip on Lena. His smile was ominous, like he knew something was coming for us. I didn't like that smile. I didn't like the bad that I knew would be coming.

That was when I saw something. No, someone swooping down like a hawk. Landing in front of us. His eyes were burning red. He yanked Lena from my arms. I tried to hold her, but he was stronger. Theo. That was his name. The green haired boy.

And then she was gone from me. Theo dove into the air, taking Lena with him.

I shouted for her. Jumping in the air like an idiot for her. It was pointless; she was out of reach now. Then his voice broke through, and I couldn't take it anymore. "Looks like your only defense is gone? How does it feel to be weaker than a girl?" Aiden mocked. I stopped my unsuccessful attempt to get Lena and smiled at him with pure sarcasm.

"Actually, women can be just as strong as men. So I like standing back, watching my girl kick ass. It doesn't offend me. It doesn't scare me. Real men can handle a strong girl." He looked amused, but I wasn't finished. "But I forgot you're not a real man."

"I am a better man than you. I am a better fighter than you. She isn't here to save you now." Aiden was furious.

"You? The better man? That is truly rich, Aiden. What makes you a better man again? Is it the fact that you've brainwashed and controlled millions of people? Oh wait, is it the fact that you're a villain? I wasn't aware that villainy was the key to being a good man. I must being doing it wrong." He didn't answer. He watched on.

"You are spineless, and evil. You are cruel and heartbreaking to watch. You are so vile that you can't even see it, can you?" The crashes of the ocean seemed to add effect to my words, and I felt invincible. I walked towards Aiden. He was smiling his evil smile now.

"But that's okay. I'm not tied up. So we have a fair fight on our hands." That was when I punched his smug face. Blood flew out of his mouth as soon as the punch landed. I felt joy, pure joy rising in the pit of my stomach. My ruined hand fought as best as it could. Each punch stung, but it was worth it. "Fuck you, Aiden." I screamed as I punched him once more in the face.

His face was bloody, and he became more limp with each punch. By the end of this, I would make him just as ugly as me. Two swollen, disproportionate shaped brothers. Two lonely souls, with near nothing left to lose. Two angry, bitter brothers who hated the other for different reasons than the last.

Each blow seemed to fill me with more anger than before. I was screaming into the air. Hateful obscenities. I was a mad man. Fear was within Aiden now. I could see it in his weak eyes, as he should have been. I stopped. I had ripped the wound open on my injured hand. My knuckles bloody. Aiden beaten to a pulp.

"Have you had enough?" I screamed into his face. I had finally won. I wasn't beaten down for once, he was. To my dismay, he didn't answer. I leaned closer and realized his chest was no longer moving up and down. He wasn't breathing. I put my head to his chest. Nothing.

I stood quickly off him. He was dead. I killed him through my rage. *What have I done?*

I turned quickly away from the scene, running my hands through my hair. I killed my brother. I was a murderer. I had to remember, he was evil and he had killed many people. But now, I was just like him. Just like my father. I turned to face him again.

He wasn't on the ground anymore. "Shit." I whispered in angst.

"Over here." He slurred. I pivoted around towards his voice, but he was faster.

The punch landed on my jaw. My face was already screwed up beyond repair, so it didn't even matter to me. *Keep them coming, who cares anymore.*

That was when he tackled me to the ground. I felt the wind knock out from my lungs. I didn't know where I landed, but then I felt a breeze that was too close for comfort. When I looked beside me, I didn't see anymore ground. I was at the edge of the roof, and the ocean was directly beneath me.

I looked back up to see Aiden over top of me, holding me halfway on the roof, halfway off. Now it was my turn for Aiden to see the change in my eyes. Fear.

He stood up, hovering over me with a mocking smile. With one swift kick, he knocked me backwards. It was enough.

I was going to fall to my death, but I managed to grab the edge before I fell over. Now, I was at his mercy, and he knew it.

His eyes glowed and he looked crueler than usual because of the position I was in. "I win." He said, taking his foot, and placing it over my hand. My damaged hand. My only lifeline left was about to be cut off.

Chapter Fourteen: You Can't Hide Lena

"Let go of me," I screamed to Theo. I was thrashing in his arms but he didn't budge. "I can't leave Jared down there with him. Take me back." I shouted into his face.

Theo looked forward, and I gripped his hair until he was forced to look at me. "Take me back, damn it. Or I will rip your head off. Literally." I said through gritted teeth.

"I don't take orders from you." He said and I grunted. Ready to take action against him, but then we landed.

"What are we doing?" I screamed. I jumped to take flight into the air, but he jerked me down by my foot, slamming me into the ground. "I will murder you." I took my foot, slamming it into his head. He fell backwards. He didn't as much as look at me. He rose into the air, leaving me behind.

"What the fuck, Theo?" I shouted into the air.

That was when he shot a blast at me. The blast missed me by an inch, but I felt fury. I rose in the air to match him. We were both levitating in the air, facing off with each other. He shot another blast, but I shifted away from it at the last moment. I grunted in frustration, and held my palm in front of me, shooting him with blasts back.

The blast hit him straight on, and he was shot back. *Good riddance.* I was about to take flight into the air, when I caught sight of Theo charging through the air towards me. I braced myself for the impact.

"What was that for?" he screamed to me as he tackled me in the air, and we were flying super speed, towards the ocean. I didn't feel the burn anymore and I was surprised to find that he didn't seem feel it either. He was flying over the ocean, after all.

When we were completely over the ocean, he was whispering in my ear, faster than I had ever heard someone speak before. "We are being watched. They can't hear us once we're over the ocean because there is static, but they can see us." *Who?* I wanted to ask but he interrupted my thoughts. "Keep fighting me. Don't hurt me though." I looked at him in disbelief.

He smacked me in the back of the head for effect when I looked at him like he was crazy, and I felt like I was seeing stars. I slapped him back in anger. "Lena, the control center is underwater."

"What?" I shrieked.

He slapped a hand over my mouth and kept speaking in his hushed voice. "Keep up. I am going to throw you into the water, and you are going to act like you're drowning. I'll pretend that the water is hurting me, and faint too. I'll meet you down there." He whispered.

Before I could even answer, he took his fist and hit the back of my head so hard that I really did feel myself losing grip, and before I knew it, he was dropping me from his hands, screaming in pain as if the water really were burning him. I let my body become immobile, and hit the water with a splash.

I let myself sink down until I heard the second splash that was Theo. Finally I opened my eyes, and saw him swimming towards me. He grabbed my arm and guided me down.

We swam, and I was breathing without struggling against the ocean water. He tugged my arm, and I swam with him. My vision was heightened, but I couldn't understand what was before me. Through the water, I could see a building appearing in my vision. Then I realized that we were here.

Here.

Here being a control room right in the middle of the ocean. Under the island. Theo wasn't kidding when he said there was a control room. But controlling what?

I couldn't believe what I was seeing but Theo urged me to swim on until we were walking on the ground. *How was any of this possible?* I looked behind me to see the water, stopped by an imaginary glass. The water was beating gently in waves against that imaginary glass.

"What is this?" I said quietly, wringing the water out my shirt. The room was filled with blank computer screens. I was instantly transformed back in time. My father's lab looked just like this.

"This is the control room. This is pretty much Gabe's baby. Everything is waterproof in case something goes wrong and the water was to pile into this area. Look." He said simply, as he clicked on one of the computers. And on those computers, there were images of brains, lined with dots along each brain. Now it made sense, this was how Gabe could control each person. I reached another computer that opened the image of another brain.

"Is there a computer for each person?" I gasped.

"No. There would be a lot more computers." He said simply. "There is a computer for each region of the world. This computer holds all memories of the controlled humans, and goes right into Gabe's head. He sees everything. He knows absolutely everything. He knows every flaw you have, every memory you have. Gabe could destroy you by just knowing enough about you. Gabe is the real dangerous one, Lena. Dr. Ravana is the mastermind behind the plan, but Gabe executed every plan. Look at him now, he is the ruler of the robots, not Dr. Ravana."

I was at a loss for words, but Theo continued. "Gabe had the computers set up to keep control. The weird thing is that Dr. Ravana knows he will die soon, he keeps repeating this to Gabe. Dr. Ravana is the one who told Gabe to just transfer all the technology and control to himself."

"So, Gabe is the main enemy now." Theo just nodded at my words. "Why is no one guarding this place?" I looked around the dark room.

"No one knows it is here but Gabe and Dr. Ravana." He shrugged.

"Then how do you know?" I said quickly and a little frightened.

"I overheard them talking about the transfer many weeks ago. I was under their control, but I could still hear. Gabe had me follow him down here last week. I wasn't allowed to enter in the room. I was just made to keep guard in the water that no one followed him down here. He made a mistake thinking he would never lose control of me. He made a mistake, thinking that he could control so many people." He shrugged.

"Still. Why wouldn't he have someone guarding this place?" I asked.

"Beats me." He didn't elaborate further, and I let it go.

"How do you have control, by the way?" I asked, distracted.

"I have no idea. One minute, I was under Gabe's control. The next minute, I remembered everything."

"This could mean others are out of his grasp too, doesn't it?"

"I wish I knew." He sighed.

"I guess there are many flaws in the cure. Aren't there?" I asked Theo. He was deep in thought.

"It's a flawed idea, because too many people have will. Free will." He answered back and I stared at him. "Too many people don't want to lose their control. Too many people are sick of being treated as nothing. Too many people are fighting back. They are going to lose everything, mark my words." His voice was severe, but he was right. Humanity would win over evil, every time.

"So why did you bring me here?" I asked.

"We have lives to save. And you're the antidote. You know that, don't you?" I froze at his words.

"Do you really believe that?" I asked simply. "If I were the antidote, then the world would have been saved a long time ago. But as you see, we are worse off than where we started."

"Yes, we are worse off. We are at rock bottom, and the only way from rock bottom is up." I smiled at his words.

"But back to you being the antidote, I know it. So do you, so does Dr. Ravana and Gabe. That's why they want to capture your mind so badly. You'd screw up their whole world domination thing. Don't you think?" he laughed and I felt a giggle bubbling up but I didn't let it spill over. This wasn't the time or place for laughs.

"Now what?" I asked seriously.

"We infiltrate the system. We transfer all the information to you." I was wide eyed at the thought, but he just looked at me with a serious look on his face.

That's when I was laughing. "And what the hell would I do with this stuff? I don't even know what I'm looking at right now. I am not a super genius like Gabe. I don't know what to do if it were transferred to me."

"You would know exactly what to do." I shook my head in disbelief. "When it transfers to you, everything goes to you. All the knowledge. All of it." he said like it was the most simple thing in the world.

"How the hell would we do that?" I asked.

"Well, that's the problem, isn't it? I have no idea." I rolled my eyes.

"Then how do you know it would all transfer to me? The knowledge and all?" I asked sarcastically.

"I just know." He said simply, and he turned his back on me. I threw my hands up in confusion. This was going to be a long night.

***

After what felt like an hour of arguing and investigating, we felt hopeless. My clothes were finally drying, and I felt relief at that.

Out of nowhere, the lights died. Theo and I were in pitch black. I could see with my intensified eyesight normally, but I couldn't see a thing in here.

"Theo?" I said nervously, while searching with my hands in the dark.

"Over here." He shouted. And to my relief, he turned on a flashlight, revealing his face. I didn't know where he found the flashlight, but I was grateful. "Here." He said as he tossed the other flashlight to me.

We went back to our search. It felt like it was never ending. Nothing was jumping out at me. Nothing seemed significant to me, but it might have been the fact that I knew nothing of technology or science.

That was when the screen began speaking to us out of nowhere. We jumped at the sound simultaneously. We caught each other's eyes in fear. We had been busy searching on each computer for the "brain," as Theo called it.

"Theo. Lena." It spoke again, and we both jolted from our trances as every computer lit up once more.

"Should I answer?" I whispered to Theo, but he was busy staring at the computer screen in front of him as if he were being hypnotized.

"Hello?" I snapped in front of Theo's face, but he stayed frozen. That was when I felt panic running through my body. Chills ran over my skin and I felt like I wasn't alone. I felt like someone was behind me, watching my every move. I flashed the light behind me and to my relief, there was no one.

"Lena." The computer spoke again to me. I flashed the light back to the screen, illuminating it.

"Hello." I said quietly, brushing past Theo, who was as still a statue. "What do you want?" I felt like an idiot. Here I was, savior of the world or so they say, talking to a computer.

Silence followed. My mouth was dry and I felt like the air in the room was getting warmer. "Hello?" I said one more time. That was when the lights went blank. All of the computers shut down at once, accompanied by the sound of a zap.

I gasped and then I was running through the aisles, checking each computer. Every screen was blank and I felt like I could cry. Would Theo wake up? Or would I be alone in this once more?

That was when the alarm sounded. "Intruder alert. Intruder." It blasted.

"No." I screamed. I started slamming my hands on the keyboard in front of me, willing it to turn back on. "Come on. Come back on now." I shouted over the blare of the alarm.

And then by some magic, one did. In the corner of the room. I went dashing over to the computer light. "Theo." I shouted to see if he would follow. He was still unmoving. It was comical, and yet freaky. I turned away from him because I couldn't stand to see him that way. I stuffed the flashlight in my back pocket.

The light intensified as I placed my hands on the keyboard of the computer. Then a new light appeared. It was green, and it seemed to scan my entire body with its beam. As soon as the beam was gone, I found out that I was frozen, just as Theo was.

This was a feeling I was so accustomed to now. Dr. Ravana, Gabe, Aiden, had all trapped me within my own body countless times. I couldn't speak, I couldn't move. I didn't feel panic. I waited for the feeling to subside. I didn't even worry that someone would come to get me in my petrified state. That was what they had done to me. Fear had strengthened me. My enemies had toughened me.

A second passed before I could feel myself blinking once more. As soon as I had the power to move, the computer dinged. *Dinner's ready?* I backed away from the computer as it spoke once more. "Welcome Lena." It said loudly. "We have been waiting for you."

We? I felt myself backing up before I could stop myself. That was when I felt something hit my back. I lunged forward, ready to fight whomever it was, but then he spoke. "Lena?" Theo asked curiously.

"Oh, Theo. Thank god. Are you okay? I thought I lost you there." He was looking at me thoughtfully when the alarm sounded again. I hadn't noticed that it had even stopped.

I saw just in time that the computer in the corner was shutting down now. "Why did it scan me? And why did it say they were waiting for me if it was just going to shut down again?" I asked peculiarly. Theo looked at me as if he were confused.

That was when red lights started flickering and a second alarm started blaring in the distance. "We? Let's not wait to find out who we is. Let's get the hell out of here." Theo shouted, grabbing my hand, but I stopped him.

"But we didn't accomplish anything. We are still four steps behind."

"We have to go." He screamed over the roar of the alarm.

I looked back at the computers. He was right. They were all shut down. The answers would remain within them. Failure should just come in a form that looked exactly like me.

He tugged my hands once more, and then we were running. I saw the wall ahead of me and I could see the water within in. It was amazing to see the technology used by Gabe to keep the ocean separate from the room with computers. His talents were used for evil though, so it was hardly worth admiring.

When we hit the water, it was freezing, I felt my throat constrict from the chill. I began to swim but before I could take my first stroke, I was grabbed around the ankle. There was a tug on my leg, but then there was a jerk. A sharp, harsh pull that didn't come from Theo. Panicking, I turned and punched whatever was behind me. Theo was there in an instant, taking the gun from his waistband and shooting whatever or whomever it was that I couldn't see. I paddled back to the room, and fell against the floor.

Theo landed beside me, gasping for air. "Stairs. Go up the stairs." He shouted to me.

I stumbled forward, my clothes clinging to my body again. I looked frantically for the stairs. *Where were the stairs even at?* Theo shoved me towards the backside of the room, and what appeared to be a dark room, held stairs.

"Where the hell does this lead?" I screamed as I climbed the steps.

"No idea." Theo shouted to me. That was when we both were found motionless at the sound we heard. Screeching was coming from the bottom of the stairs. We looked at each other, wide eyed.

"Theo, what do we do?" I whispered quickly, and he kept his wide-eyed gaze, ignoring my words.

He looked so frightened. One of us had to take charge, and it looked like it had to be me. "We're strong. We can do this. Don't be afraid." He swallowed deeply, and I urged him by pulling his hand the way he pulled me on just moments before. The screeching didn't stop. We ran full speed up the stairs, into the darkness. The staircase felt never ending. When we finally reached the door at the top, I almost sighed with relief. I jerked the knob. Locked. It was locked. I pulled, and thrashed about frantically. This was our only way out. Below was something unknown. Something dark and terrifying.

The screeching was closer than ever now, and I turned to face it. Theo jerked away from the sound, accidentally knocking his head into the wall. I grabbed his hand and jerked him up off the ground, rubbing his cheek to comfort him.

"Are you with me?" I asked. He nodded and I sighed. "We got this. Face this with me." I said.

"Together?" he didn't have time to nod, the screeching was right in our faces now.

Chapter Fifteen: There's Nowhere to Run
Jared

By some grace of God, I was hanging on still. Aiden's foot was pressed into my knuckles, my bloody knuckles that had just beaten his face in, but I didn't let go. He was shouting obscenities to me, but I couldn't hear them any longer. The pain seemed to drown out everything but my thoughts. I was deep in thought of a plan to escape. I had a will to live. I had to save Lena from whatever Theo was doing to her.

As he shouted, blood rolled down his face and splashed onto mine. I was a bloody mess already, but I didn't want to add his tainted blood on me either.

He lifted his foot of mine, and that precious second of relief was perfect, but then he slammed his foot right back down on my knuckles. I groaned out. I longed for a time when I wouldn't know this pain anymore. *By the end of this night would I even be able to feel pain, or would I be immune to it all?*

"Jared." Aiden said through clenched teeth. "Either I am going to kill you, or someone else will. No one wants you alive. You do realize that, don't you?" I didn't answer. I didn't have to. It was a fact that everyone wanted me dead, but the truth was that I wanted everyone dead in return.

It would be so simple to forget the world but there was too much to do. It didn't need saving. It needed retribution. I would be that vengeance. I would be the one to serve justice. I was the only one left who could.

I was trying as hard as I could to keep myself up. I felt weak and empty inside. I didn't know where Lena could be. Did Gabe or Holland finally catch up to her? Gabe. *Of course.* Gabe had given me so many gadgets to use before I left to find Lena. I could use one. Right now.

"I'm doing you a favor." Aiden screamed at the top of his lungs. "I'm showing mercy. Everyone else has worse plans than I do for you. I would give you a quick death, you'd like that, wouldn't you?" he asked.

I didn't answer. I kept my head down so he couldn't see my expression. He couldn't see an idea growing in my head. I didn't meet his eyes, a sign of defeat to him, but I was ready.

I watched the waves below me. I could not fall to the death trap below. The waves slammed against the building. If I were to fall right now, the waves would slam me against the building. I wouldn't be able to swim against the current.

"Answer me." he demanded. "Say something." He pressed his foot deeper on my wounded hand, I felt the bite of pain but I didn't look up still.

"Look, I can do this the easy way, and let you fall to your death. Or I can pull you up, fight you like a man, and then throw you over the edge. You decide."

That was when I finally looked up. I had one chance to do this right. My good hand was on the trigger. "I think I'd like to fight you like a man." I took Gabe's extender out. The gadget was used to extend and reach things in high places. It looked exactly like a tiny pencil when held in my hand, but when I pushed it open, it became a long pole. It nailed Aiden right in the face, causing him to stumble back, holding his nose in shock. His foot released my hand, and I hoisted myself up with the little strength I had.

Aiden was on me in an instant. I was still close to the edge, so I jumped over to the side. "You can't use your little toys forever. What will you do when they run out?" Aiden cried while holding his nose.

"I don't need those toys to kick your ass." I said though I felt weaker than I ever had. The beatings, the holding on to the edge were catching up to me.

His hand was heading right for my face, but I gripped his hand with all my might, forcing him away. I took my foot and pushed against his gut, until he fell to the ground. I was on him immediately. For the second time tonight, I punched with everything I had, all the hate I carried inside me, I unleashed it on his face. Blood spluttered from his nose, his mouth, even his ears. Then I stopped.

That was when I heard it. Sirens.

"What is that?" I shouted to Aiden. He didn't move an inch. It was as if he couldn't hear the blares.

"Alarm." He whispered finally.

"No shit, alarm. Why the hell are they going off?" I shouted.

He shifted his head slightly, and whispered, "Infiltrated." And then he was out. Let's hope he would stay out this time.

I got off him quickly, what the hell was happening? I went to stand on the edge to overlook the building. Inside, red lights were flickering on and off.

Where was Lena? Was this her doing? Theo?

I looked back to Aiden. He wasn't there. *Damn it.* I turned my back for a second. Rule number one, never let your guard down. Ever. And I had done it twice in the same night. Why was I so stupid?

I looked to my right. He was slumped over, but he had my extender in his hand. "You choose the hard way. Here it is." Before I could speak, or even think, he pressed the go button.

I felt the hit before I could comprehend it. Then I was flying through the air. Off the building. I could swim, but the waves pounded below me. It would swallow me up, until there was nothing left of me.

Chapter Sixteen: You Can't Run
Lena

THEIR RED EYES gleamed in the darkness, staring me down. I couldn't afford to be afraid. Fear would lead to my death. I wasn't human entirely, neither was Theo. Neither was the person whose red eyes were looking at me.

We were equal, but one of us had to win. Theo's hand was still in mine. We had to get down the stairs to swim to the shore, because the door behind us wouldn't open. It wouldn't lead us to safety. Safety was past these red eyes.

Then the face in front of me screeched again. I had never heard such screeching sounds in my life. I had seen some creepy things in my lifetime now, but this was unbelievably peculiar. I took my flashlight from my back pocket, and shined the light in the face of the screeching monster in front of me. I nearly dropped the flashlight. This time, I did feel fear because of what I saw. I was shaking, and the light was flickering on and off his face.

The face before me was Max. My previous next-door neighbor. He was almost completely devoid of any human feature. The skin on one side of his face was gone. One side of his face was metal, and the other was human skin. His eyes were red, and his left eye bulged out from the metal.

"Max?" I said gently, reaching my hand out to comfort him, and maybe remind him that it was me, Lena, his neighbor for fifteen years. His hand jerked out with supersonic speed, and he grabbed hold of my hand. He held it there. Not moving, not screeching.

Theo spoke up slowly. "Gabe's new system wipes out all human characteristics. He's gone, Lena. He is lost. Let him go."

I jerked my hand away, but he held it tightly. It felt like I'd be stuck there forever. "I am not holding him. He is holding me." I whispered feverishly back. I looked down to see that his entire body was metal. He was a full on robot. The only skin remaining was the half face he had. It was a futile attempt, but I had to try. I used my eyes to burn through his metal to make him let go of my hand.

He screeched and punched me right in the gut. I flew backwards, hitting the door behind me as I went. There was a loud snap as I fell to the floor. The door still didn't open, even though the crash was fierce.

I held my arm in slight pain. Something had to have broke by the impact. I lifted my shirt up to see the damage. My rub bone was protruding through my skin. I gritted my teeth, already seeing the skin closing around the wound. I was healing. I pushed the bone in with a cry. Blood poured down until it stopped completely. The wound was healed. I never clicked the button in my necklace to turn myself back into a human, thankfully.

I jerked myself off the ground. Max was screeching in Theo's face, ready to punch him too. Theo was unprepared when the blow landed on his face. He lurched through the air and into the door, slamming his head. "Theo." I cried out, but he popped up quickly, unharmed.

"I have had enough of you." I screamed and to my surprise, green encircled my body. My scream seemed to echo through the stairwell. My necklace lifted off my chest, and I grabbed Theo to move behind me. I didn't know how I knew, but I knew. I knew exactly what to do in this moment, to defeat Max.

Max cowered down by my fury. As the scream stopped echoing, he screeched at us, revealing bloodstained razor sharp teeth. That was when I saw many others just like him joining behind him. This was it.

They were right in our faces and that was when I unleashed my power. I pushed my hands forward, and screamed once more like a banshee. I felt Theo hovering behind me, gripping my shirt in what I could only guess was panic.

The power behind my hands was extraordinary. The entire stairwell lit a bright green, before it was blown into obliteration. The only ones protected in my bubble were Theo and I. The screams died down, and Theo and I were the only two left in sight.

"What the fuck was that?" he screamed in my ears. His voice was shaky. *Was he afraid of me?*

At the end of his sentence, a rumble began beneath our feet. The sound was deafening as it sounded as if the entire place would cave in. One thing was for sure that the staircase was going to collapse at any moment.

"No idea. Let's get a move on." We ran past the ash, which were bodies of robots just moments before. Some eyeballs were on the floor, still twitching. I tried not to look at that.

The staircase kept rumbling and I finally reached the bottom, but Theo was not there. "Theo!" I shouted. He was on the bottom step, when it collapsed.

The floor continued to rumble beneath me. If I didn't move fast, I would fall under too, but I couldn't leave Theo alone. I soared into the air, searching the wreckage.

"Theo?" I shouted in to the air. "Please be okay." Thank god I was in the air, because the floor began to crumble. My powers were too strong for me. I was destroying everything. The walls were spider cracking along the wall. Everything was collapsing.

"Theo." I screamed once more. The ceiling started caving in. I couldn't leave Theo though. He saved me on the roof. He was my friend. He risked it all for me.

That was when I soared where the stairs had just collapsed. Underneath was rubble everywhere. I didn't see him anywhere.

That was when more debris fell. Closing the hole that I had just flown through. "Crap." I whispered under my breath. "Theo?" I shouted into the darkness. That was when a groan answered me. "Theo?" I screamed in return. I followed the moans.

When I reached him, he was under a lot of the wreckage. "I can't lift it off of me. I have strength and I can't even use it. Why?" He said as he tried to lift the fragments off of him.

"Stop moving for a second." I was looking to find what held him in place. I lifted the first piece of cement off of him. I found the culprit. Theo had his shirt stuck under cement blocks.

I moved it quickly and he tried to stand, but couldn't. What was going on? More pieces of ceiling fell on us each moment we stayed there. I took the blows, breaking them with my fist. I had to get us out of here.

That was when I saw it. Theo's leg. Protruding through his skin, was a giant nail. The nail was glued to the ground. I ripped his pant leg open, to see that the nail had healed inside his leg.

"Theo. This is going to hurt." I didn't give him time to ask what or why. I just lifted his leg off the nail quickly. He screamed in pain, but his leg was already on its way to being healed.

I looked up to find that the hole in the ceiling was completely exposed. The invisible wall seemed to have dropped with the explosion, allowing the water in. It pounded down on us at full force.

"Let's go!" I shouted to him before we were crushed in the face with ocean water. He seemed to be in a state of shock because he remained frozen after I pulled his leg free. I grabbed him quickly up. We began swimming together against the pounding of ocean water on our heads.

Theo was fine, but he was swimming slower than he had before. It was driving me crazy, so I grabbed his arm and did all the work until we reached the shore.

As soon as we broke our heads through, I let out a sigh. Gabe's control center was destroyed.

"We destroyed his control system room." I said simply.

Theo looked at me with a funny look on his face.

"What?" I asked staggered.

"Lena, if it were that simple. I would have blown the place up last week."

"Then what just happened? The water destroyed everything."

"Lena, the control room isn't damaged."

"I am confused." I felt like my head was spinning.

"The computers revive themselves. They're advanced. Hello, Gabe created them. The invisible wall will restore itself, and there will be no water damage. Go back down and see yourself if you don't believe me." he pointed down.

"Then why did we have to escape so quickly?" I was at a loss for anything else.

"It would have rebuilt on top of us. We would have died." He shrugged.

"Well now what should we do?" I screamed to Theo. He was too distracted to hear me. He was pointing in the air. I followed his hand, until my gaze fell on top of the roof.

Aiden was beside Jared with a sort of pole in his hands. He lunged for Jared and that was it.

Then I was screaming in denial. Jared went flying through the air, and I shot out of the water and into the air in an instant. Theo shouted to me, gripping my hand harshly. "No. You can't do this. You're too important to the world." He screamed in my ear but I jerked free of his hold, and I kept going.

I flew through the air to reach Jared, to save him, but I felt a large hand on mine, pulling me severely back to the ground. "Let go, Theo." When he didn't let go, I whipped sharply around only to find it was Joseph. He punched me sharp in the nose. I felt like I had gotten whiplash from the impact.

Jared was falling through the air towards the ocean to my left. I was screaming for him. I had to use my power, to get rid of Joseph. I took my hands out, ready to destroy everything in my path until I could reach Jared. I pointed them directly at the glass building.

"Theo. Duck." I screamed through my teeth.

I screamed as my necklace pulled from my chest once more to glow emerald. The entire glass building shattered around me, the glass freezing in the air at my command. I took my hands towards Joseph.

Every piece of glass was flying right towards his face. Shards of glass pierced the sand but more importantly, pierced Joseph's face. He stood shocked, but I didn't get the pleasure of seeing the glass pierce his entire body.

I didn't see glass stab his eyes, puncture his heart, or destroy his insides. They were already rotten like the disease he put in so many humans. I had too much to do than to watch him die, but I knew he would die. He was human, after all. I searched the sky endlessly for him, hoping he had used a jet pack, or was still mysteriously falling through the air. When I reached the building, he was gone.

"Jared." I cried towards the water. I flew in circles above the water. The waves crashed viciously. Jared was lost to the waves. I couldn't find him anymore.

I landed on the roof in a rush, to find Aiden, to kill Aiden, but he was nowhere to be found just as Jared was gone as well.

I felt the world collapsing around me. I had to be better for him. I had to stay in control. I had to beat them. They couldn't win. Not anymore.

Chapter Seventeen: Bad Dream
Jared

I saw her. She simply lifted her hands in front of her face, and then she screamed. She blew up the entire building, only taking the glass with her. I saw her as she pushed the spikes of glass right into Joseph's face. There was no stopping her. There was no way to stop the imminent either. He was dead. He had to be dead. Shards of glass puncturing every part of the body would leave no survivors.

Theo was pushed deep into the sand, and was completely unaffected by the debris. It happened so fast that I almost forgot I was falling through the air, until I hit the glass. Nope, it wasn't glass. It was freezing cold water.

The water sloshed all around my body, pushing me against the rocks to the side. It felt like I was being stabbed with glass myself. I swam against the waves, but the waves were too rough. I was a fragile man after all. I was no match to the beast that was the waves.

My body was slammed against the rocks, and I tried to push against it but I just couldn't. I had to fight for my life. Lena could take care of herself, this much I knew, but I couldn't bear to leave her. I couldn't let the waves win. There was too much that I needed to do. There was too much to live for.

I had said it all night. Let them win or let them kill me, but this time it was different. I had so much to live for. We all did. This world was cruel and ruthless, but there was also love. It was all I had in this world. It was all anyone had to live for, and it was enough.

That was when I heard her scream. It carried throughout the water to me, and I felt a shove against me in the water. The push was enough, because I slammed against the rocks once more, but it didn't stop there.

Instantly, I was thrust underneath the rocks. I hadn't prepared. I hadn't taken a deep breath. My panic was already drowning me. I was swallowing so much water. It would be amazing if I didn't die right there.

I pushed against the rocks that were now above my head. I was just losing oxygen faster with each heave. I couldn't push the rocks out of the way.

That was when a gush of water swirled around me, until I was pulled further under water. I tried to fight and swim up, but the gush was tugging me down. Down. Down.

I felt my air becoming less and less. I tried not to panic, so I could keep my oxygen just a little bit longer. I had no way to get back to the surface, because the rocks were above my head now. I tried to swim to the side again, but there was no use. The water struggled against me as I tried to swim back to the top.

I let my body sink with the gushes. I fought as hard as I could, and it just wasn't enough. That was when I felt like I was falling through the air. I screamed, and I could hear it.

How can I hear myself scream under water? Was I already dead? Was this heaven? That was when I felt air. *Smack.* I harshly slammed to the ground.

I could breathe. I was no longer in the water. I gasped for air and coughed, spitting out water. I looked around me. I was underground. I was in a sort of safe house. *Under the island? How was this possible at all?* I knew instantly that this was all Gabe's doing.

He could make anything possible. You imagine it, and Gabe could create it.

I glanced up to see the ocean was above me. It looked as if glass was holding the water in. Computers were all around me. They were all blank screened, and the alarm was still blaring. Red lights flickered on and off. This reminded me of the room to get into our safe house on the beach.

In the corner of the dark room, a computer flickered on, illuminating the face of someone in the corner.

I jumped at the sight. "Who's there?" I shouted. *What a cliché to yell that out to a figure in the dark, genius. Way to be original.* No one spoke and I knew I had to get out of here. I stumbled backward, falling. My feet had toppled over from a large lump on the ground. I moved it with my foot, and screamed at the sight of two bloody eyeballs staring up at me.

I continued my scream fest, as I backed away on my hands and feet, only to stumble across more ash, and more eyeballs. *What happened here?* "They're dead." A voice spoke to me.

Clearly they're dead. "Who is there?" I screeched again.

"Well, I can be your greatest nightmare, or your savior. Your choice." She said without a hint of sarcasm. She revealed herself in the room.

Panic filled my lungs. It was Lena, but just as soon as she was Lena, she was someone else. Black hair that was parted in the middle that blocked out most of her face. She was fairly thin.

"Lena? What is going on?" I said, and she stood from the chair in the corner. Revealing her face even more in the computer light.

She walked slowly towards me and I felt my heart quickening. I could easily take her, but there was something so familiar.

"Lena?" I said calmly.

The black haired girl transformed once more into my beautiful girl. Lena.

"How are you doing that?" *I didn't think her powers included turning into other people?*

"I have my ways." She responded bashfully.

"Wow. You continue to amaze me." I briefly stroked her cheek, but she turned quick from my grasp. "How did you find me so fast? You were just on the roof?" I asked quickly.

"Tell me what you've found down here." She smiled at me, ignoring my question, and I had forgotten it as soon as she smiled. I couldn't help but grin back.

"I know Gabe is behind this, he has to be. Remember the safe house? The layout is almost identical."

"Gabe, of course. Alec could never come up with this stuff." She said.

"Alec? You mean Dr. Ravana, my father? I have never heard you call him Alec before." I said skeptically.

Her face was in a deep frown but she quickly smiled and recovered. "Of course. I meant Dr. Ravana." I couldn't shake the feeling that something was different about her.

"So weird to hear you call him that. That's all."

"Sorry." She kept walking around the room, observing each computer. "So what would Gabe make these computer do then?" She asked.

"Gabe was a very organized man. For example, he might have each brain mapped out here." I stopped for a second. "No. This place probably is the main control system. Gabe would never leave it out in the open. Hence why we are down here, at the bottom of the ocean. What is strange to me is that he doesn't have the place guarded very well. Maybe this place is a secret and no one knows about it." My mind was going a mile a minute, but I couldn't stop. Lena watched on with hunger in her eyes.

I continued, "Gabe must have all the answers in here. He has to. And only one person can answer to it." A thought came to my mind at that moment. "Lena, we have to transfer this software to you."

She smiled nervously. "Me? Why me?" she laughed a hesitant chuckle, and I frowned.

"The system can be yours to control. You are the answer. You are the antidote. You know this." I was about to point to her neck but stopped myself when I was her necklace was gone.

Butterflies entered my stomach. This wasn't Lena. She wouldn't ever part with her necklace, not even when she was under control. "Lena, where is your necklace?" Maybe I shouldn't have asked, maybe I shouldn't have revealed that I knew she was an imposter, but the damage was done.

Lena's hand quickly reached for the necklace, and came up short. "Oh no! Where is my necklace?" she asked in an aggravated tone.

"You lost it?" I said in disbelief.

"Yes, I must have lost it. I bet I left it on my nightstand." That was when I knew she was lying. The necklace had just lit up green, as the real Lena blew up the building, killing Joseph.

"Ah. We will find it, don't worry." I couldn't let her know that I knew the truth. I had to keep the charade up.

"Let's get to looking at these monitors, shall we?" I asked quickly.

I didn't see it coming, but the moment her knuckle met my stomach, I was sent flying across the room. Gasping for air on the ground, I could barely raise my head to meet hers.

"I have to do this. You have to stay out of the way." She said in a hurry. I blinked furiously. She grabbed the chair, and yanked me down in it. She tied the rope around my body until I couldn't move an inch. She had done it in super speed.

"Lena, why are you doing this?"

"I am not Lena." She responded quickly.

She transformed herself before me in an instant. Her coat of black hair framing her face once more. I knew she wasn't Lena, but she still looked so familiar to me.

"Who are you?" I asked weakly.

"I won't tell you my name, but I am going to clone you." I pulled against the ropes she tied me in.

"Clone me?" I panicked.

"Stay still." She said simply, and locked eyes with me. That was when I felt the greatest pain. Like my body was being split in half, and stretched at the same time. When it was over, I was staring at myself. I screamed. I screamed until she hit me upside the head, and I didn't see anymore.

Chapter Eighteen: Can't Move With Your Feet Tied
Lena

He was gone. That was all I could think about. For the millionth time, we have been separated. This time it felt pretty permanent. I was getting tired of the back and forth. I was tired of this war. I was tired of fighting for things that would never be mine again.

If Jared was truly gone, then I had nothing left to lose. I had nothing else to care about, and that meant my humanity was in the dust. This meant war. Where was Aiden? I would murder him. He and everything he loved would be turned to ash.

I heard screeches in the air, and turned midair. In the distance, I saw red glowing eyes. All the robots were flying towards me. For once, I wasn't filled with fear. They were mine to lead now anyways. They were meant to be followers, and followers of mine they would have to be. I didn't want the power to control them, but I had to do it. I had to defeat Dr. Ravana, and this was the way.

I held my hands out in front of me. By command, they froze in the air. "Who do you listen to?" I spoke directly into my necklace. The necklace was almost a loud speaker. I could hear my own voice piercing the night.

As it turned out, my necklace wasn't just a cure to being a robot; it was a control device. I was the leader of them all. I had the power that Dr. Ravana so desperately wanted. My father had played him for a fool in the end. Instead of them answering to Dr. Ravana, they answered to me now.

"Find him." I said simply, I didn't even have to speak his name. They felt my anger, and they would find him without a second thought. Each one of them turned towards the sand below. One flew down in a swift movement, snatching him up from the sand, and dropping him on his feet. Aiden was in front of me in a blink of the eye. "We meet again." I said with venom.

He turned to run, but I was faster. I landed in front of him, and the coward turned to run away again. "I can play this all day long if I have to." I shouted to his turned back. Instead of chasing him back and forth all night, I raised my arms. Every single robot that I commanded was around me in an instant. They each rose into the air. It was a sight to see, I had my arm raised in the air, and a pack of robots rose behind me with one thing on their minds, death. Death of evil. Death of corruption. Death of villainy. It was time. Aiden was dead meat.

I shot my hands forward and in an instant, the robots swarmed past me, all ready to attack. I laughed viciously at the sight of Aiden's terrified face. When they were moments from reaching him, I yelled. "Stop." They all stopped, inches from Aiden's face. He was cowered down. He was even crying.

I slowly walked my way through the rows of robots, some in the air, some beside Aiden's face, frozen in time. My heels clinking on the ground with each slow step I took. I kneeled down beside Aiden. He shrank away from me, but I jerked him up by his collar to be face to face with me. "You're free to go." I whispered and threw him to the ground. He crawled backwards but I kept walking towards him. "Tell them what you saw here. I am the master of these robots. They're mine, and the next time I see you, you will be dead."

He scrambled to his feet, running full speed away from me. I cackled into the air. I was a woman unhinged. The robots all went to their manual positions. Surrounding me, their leader.

***

I contemplated my next move. I didn't know what I wanted to do. I was just waiting for someone to come up on the roof, to face me, but no one came. Were they afraid? Or were they just one step ahead of me?

I had to stay ahead of them. I had to win for Jared. I had to give him justice. My love was too deep for him. I would kill them all, but I wanted to put the fear of God in them first and foremost.

That was when I felt a presence. I found her strawberry blonde hair swaying towards me. Disgusting. She disgusted me now. Jared wasn't here to make me forgive, or even make me be kind to her ever again. Her face was clear of all disease. It must have been all a sham.

"Well, well, well. What have we here?" She said in her annoyingly cheerful voice. I smirked.

"Holland, enough with the beating around the bush. Why are you here?"

"I am here to get my robots back under my control." She said simply with a shrug.

"Your control? I think you mean Gabe's control, right?"

She gave me a dry expression. "Yes, I meant Gabe's control, but he is too busy to come get them himself."

"Oh yes, world domination is very burdening. He had to send the helpless liar to get the robots. The whole point of world domination is to make sure things are getting done the right way."

"I am very capable. Since you scared Aiden, he won't come near you." She rolled her eyes, but I felt pleasure knowing I had scared that man. "Gabe had to bring his second hand woman, aka me, to get the job done." She was so delighted with herself but it was sickening to me.

"Go ahead and try." I waved my hands towards the robots. They were mine to control. I didn't want to control them, I didn't want to be their leader, but I was for now. It was the only way to stay a player in this game.

She lifted a hand. I had a plan. I would let ten robots go to her, so she believed she had control, and then I would have them turn on her. They were under my control, and after I freed them, they would never be controlled again.

I allowed ten to go forward to her. I put on my best face. "Oh no." I whimpered. I wanted to laugh, but that would blow my cover.

"Oh yes, Lena. They aren't yours to control. They're mine, they're Gabe's and they are Dr. Ravana's. This little plot to beat us, would never work. This is child's play to us." She was smirking, and I wanted to wipe the smirk from her face once and for all.

She raised another hand, and I let ten more come over. "You're just so much better than me, Holland." I cried in false defeat into my hands. She was licking it up.

She froze as if a voice were talking to her. "Gabe is on his way up. You can kiss your mind goodbye too." Someone did speak into her ear, Gabe. She smiled to me and I waited. I didn't frown at the thought instead I felt determination. I waited for Gabe. The main event was just beginning.

Gabe finally approached. Darkness circling his face as his red eyes protruded in the shadows. Gloom and obscurity surrounded him wherever he went. Gabe wasn't even a person anymore; he was a feeling. He was a feeling of hate, anger and sadness wrapped in one.

And boy, was he angry. His hands were shaking in the dim light. His face was red as it often was when he was pissed. "Lena, release all the robots to me, and no one gets hurt." I heard a scuffle coming from behind Gabe, and saw that he was dragging what looked like a bag behind him. I squinted my eyes until I could clearly see a figure. That was when I saw his squared jaw, and wavy dirty blonde hair. I would find him anywhere. I felt like the world was crashing, and renewing at the same time. I thought I lost him forever, and there he was, looking every bit as the man I loved.

"Let Jared go." I shouted in shock. At the sound of my voice, his eyes darted open and he reached for me with his spare hand. Gabe quickly grabbed it and jerked him up.

"Release those robots from your control and I won't hurt him." By the end of the sentence, he held a syringe right by Jared's neck. I hadn't anticipated Jared being here. I had thought he had drowned in the sea.

You are most powerful when you have nothing to lose, and now I had something to lose again. Jared was my everything. He was my will to live, to fight, to try, and now I had to keep him safe once more.

"I will release them only if you bring Jared to my side." I said through gritted teeth.

"Release them. I don't make deals with you." He said simply, pushing the syringe closer to Jared's neck. I sucked in my breath. *What was in that syringe? Could it be the disease?*

"I won't release them until you let him go. Now." I screamed in anger.

"When will you learn that I don't give a shit about what happens to you? I don't care what you think you have to offer me, because the truth is that you have nothing to offer me, Lena."

"I have everything to offer you. You think I will give you these robots. You are full of anger. You are a scared little boy on the inside, and I hold the power over you now." I screamed.

"Oh, you hold the power. I think I hold the power in between my hands right now. I hold the man who holds power over you." He said simply. He was right, but I was right too.

"I hold your entire plan in my hands right now. They don't answer to you, try to command them, they won't listen." I smirked.

"You're right." He shrugged, "then I have nothing to lose." He said as he pushed the syringe into Jared's neck, he whimpered in response.

The scream that erupted from me was inhuman. It was eerie, loud and chilling. Gabe covered his ears, while releasing Jared until he fell to the ground, grabbing his neck.

I was full of anger and fury. "What did you give him?" My voice bombed over the alarms. I was the only sound you could hear anymore.

"The disease, Lena. You have lost. Now give me my robots." Gabe said. He wasn't even frightened, but he would be.

"You think you'll get a single one of them now?" I screeched, as I flew in the air. I whipped my head towards Holland.

"Leave her alone." Gabe said. Ah, first ounce of fear, and it was for the witch with strawberry blonde hair. I struck the nerve.

I ordered the robots beside Holland to yank her up. My twenty robots, that I had let Holland think she had, flew to my side in an instant.

"Let her go." Gabe's red eyes glowered but I wanted them to feel pain.

"Hold her over the ocean." I said simply, and my robot held her by the neck. She chocked in his clutches. "I will kill her and feel absolutely nothing. That is what you have done to me." I screamed into the night. "You have made me lose everything humane about myself. Everything good about me has disappeared because of your selfish need to rule. To rule what?" My shouts intensified with my anger. I heard Holland's gasps for air as I made my robot release some hold of her neck.

"I will kill her. I will kill you. I will kill anything that stands in my way. They deserve to be free. Free of you, and your malicious ways."

He didn't say anything but smiled darkly at me. I continued my speech.

"They are mine. They will kill you, and then I will set them free." I shouted. Every robot rose up with me and I felt my eyes burning into Gabe's. He didn't look frightened anymore, and that unsettled me.

That was when robots rose behind Gabe. *Where did they come from? And how were there robots not under my control?* "I don't need them. You can have your pathetic bunch of robots. I have more robots in my control, and they're stronger." Gabe shouted, getting level with me in the air.

I would have to find out, it was either fight or die. I choose fighting. "Attack." I screamed to my robots, as I flew my hands forward. This was war.

I ordered my robot to drop Holland to the sea, and she flew down in a crash. She landed on the side of the wall, holding on for dear life. I wished the bitch had fallen in.

The sound of a thousand car crashes erupted in the air between us. Metal clashed, metal burned. There was not one person who wasn't in a fight.

I was about to join, when I remembered Jared on the ground. I rushed to Jared's side on the ground. He was heaving for air. There was already rot along his arms, and I held my breath. How the tables had turned. "I have you. I will keep you safe." I whispered. I brought my lips to his. "We got this." He heaved. He couldn't even speak. "Stay here." I stood quickly; my Jared should have just drowned in the sea because this pain was too much to see.

I searched amongst the fight to find Gabe. Of course he wasn't fighting, instead he stood still, watching me from afar. His red eyes bore into mine and I into his. I was going to kill him with my bare hands. "Jared, I will be back." I whispered without looking back.

I shot over to him, but before I could mark him, Holland stood before me. "I see you made it, what a shame. Now get out of my way, bitch." I taunted. She smiled simply and punched my stomach. I laughed viciously. "You're a tiny little human, I can kill you with one look." I said as I met her eyes. I was so angry that I knew the blast would be painful. She crumbled before me, and I cackled. "See what I mean. You're weak, Holland."

Before I could do more, I felt a knock on the back of my head. I turned quickly to see Gabe behind me. He held a gun. He must have pistol-whipped me, and I didn't even feel it. "That was a very futile attempt," I said as I met his nose with my fist. The blood pouring from his nose was very satisfying.

"You won't survive a shot to the head." he said simply, and I giggled.

"Try it." Before the words were out, he fired. I felt the slight knock. I groaned in annoyance. I felt the bullet in my forehead, my skin already closing around it. I tugged on the shell until it landed in my palm.

"Gabe. Oh, Gabe." I mocked as I walked towards him. "You made me, and you couldn't remember that you made me indestructible." I shouted to him, but he was in shock. His whole body was shaking, and he backed up with each step I took towards him.

"No. Shots to the head are your only weakness. No, there must be a flaw somewhere in your system." He was at the edge of the building now, two more steps and he would be toast. He stopped moving, and stared down my neck. I would have been convinced that he was staring at my cleavage but then I remembered my necklace was there.

He lunged forward, jerking my necklace. "What the hell?" I screamed. The robots fighting in the air stopped slightly.

"No, keep going." I yelled towards them and they continued on.

"Holland." Gabe screamed. "Help me get this necklace off her neck. Now."

Holland jumped into action, jumping on my back. She clawed at my neck, scratched at my face, pulled my hair.

That was when the weight from her dropped finally. "Well, this fight is certainly not fair." His voice whispered through the air and I felt chills. I knew that voice anywhere. It sent my heart into overdrive every time. It was buried so deep inside my heart that I would never forget the sound even if I tried to.

I whipped around quickly to meet his face. Jared held a gun to Holland's head. He had rope around his wrists. What was that about? Gabe let go of my necklace, and backed away holding his hands up.

Where rot had been leading down his arms just moments before was clear. He was still in his jeans, combat boots and white bloody tee shirt, but something was different. Jared's body was free of all rot. He was back to normal, but how?

"How did you get better so fast?" I looked towards the ground where Jared had been laying. There was no one there.

"Lena, what are you talking about?" He looked slightly irritated, but his eyes were still full of love for me. I didn't answer, but nodded for him to continue.

"How are you disease free?" Gabe asked in awe.

Before anyone had time to respond, I felt a whoosh behind me, and turned quickly away from Jared. Theo came up behind Gabe in a headlock. "Theo." I said with a sigh of relief.

"Was waiting for the perfect moment to make my grand entrance." He said with a smile. I felt nothing but relief, my two main men, and they were both okay.

All of the sudden, I was coughing and gasping for air. There was a thick layer of black smoke all around us. I couldn't see a thing, but I needed to feel Jared to know he was still here. "Jared." I cried as I reached for him and felt his familiar hand on mine. I lunged forward for Theo, gripping his hand in mine too.

The smoke made it hard for me to breathe. I felt the smoke filling up my lungs and deeming my efforts to breathe useless. I searched my eyes around, but I was coming up short. There was nothing I could see. I only held Theo and Jared's hands as if they were the only thing keeping me alive. The smoke began to clear, and I saw a man approaching us. Careful in his movements.

He spoke crisply, sounding out every syllable. "I think it's time to stop this parade, Lena. You and your band of robots have killed enough of mine. Release them to me." It was Dr. Ravana. His voice was spooky against the smoke. That tumble in the hallway must not have stopped him for long.

I gasped for air, but I spoke against the heaving in my chest. "This isn't over. This is just the beginning." I felt both of my hands being ripped away from my men, as I felt two hands jerk me up.

"Lena." I heard Jared gasp. He had been holding on to me as if I was his lifeline too, and now I was gone.

"This is over, Lena." He spat in my face as he said each word. He jerked my necklace from my neck. I felt my power leaving my body as he threw me to the ground. My salvation was gone.

Chapter Nineteen: The Message
Lena

My body was immobile. I heard the shouts. I heard the screams. I was out of control of my own body once more. This shit was getting old. I wanted to scream to them that I was still here; I was just trapped and controlled once more. How many times could a girl go under?

Jared was screaming my name over and over again. He was all I could hear now. I didn't hear commands; nor could I hear Gabe in my head, or Dr. Ravana. I just saw blankness. It was as if my eyesight had disappeared.

The necklace was gone, and everything about me seemed to have disappeared without it around my neck. I could hear the fight continue. Jared was no longer shouting for me. He was distracted. I heard

164

the smacks of punches, the breaking of robotic parts. No one bothers with me. They just left me in my corner. I was a robot, forgotten. I waited for someone to dust me off and use me against me friends, my family, and worst of all, my love.

I could hear Jared's grunts as he was fighting something I couldn't see. I wanted to protect him, but I couldn't now. I was stiff armed, while I waited for control to reenter my body.

"Lena." Something whispered around my head. I couldn't see anything. Just darkness. "Lena, open your eyes." It whispered. I heard a snap and opened my eyes at the sound.

When I opened my eyes, I was facing my mother.

"Lena." She said humbly, but it was enough to bring tears to my eyes. She seems to be in a daze, and I blinked franticly.

"Mom? Is that you?" She simply nodded and I felt my heart swell. "How are you here?"

"I am here to show you the truth." She willed me to follow her. I did. I would go wherever she went.

"You have been so brave. I can't tell you enough." She turned to smile at me but I didn't feel up to smiling. "You're upset. It will be okay." She turned back and hurried on her path.

"Your father will be happy to see you. He didn't know if you would make it to this point."

"Father? Where is he? Where are we? What is the point of this?" The questions were pouring out but she kept walking, and ignored most of what I was saying.

"Mom?" I said irritated as she kept walking down the long hallway.

"We're here." She said simply and pointed to a long table, urging me to take a seat.

She sat across from me, and then he appeared.

"Dad?" I smiled bigger than I ever had before. "It's really you. Why are you here?" He just looked at me.

"Mom wouldn't tell me either, but it is good to see you. Finally see you again." I added quickly.

"Lena, you are doing so well. I couldn't be more proud of you." He was beaming at me.

"Dad, I got controlled, yet again." I said sadly.

"You did what I wanted you to do. I want them to think they're winning. You have opened the necklace. You have unlocked the full potential of the necklace. It answers to only you, and those you love. It is in the possession of someone you hate. That necklace is smarter than you think. It knows when someone wants to use it for ill intentions. It can feel heart. It can feel fear. It can feel everything a human can feel. I created it to only answer to those who have good intentions, good heart and kind motives."

"So what does this all mean?" I asked confused.

"It means that Dr. Ravana, Gabe, Joseph, Max, the list goes on. None of them can use that necklace. It will not answer to them. We have to find a way to get that necklace back on your neck."

"I thought I finally gained control. Even if we win at this war, I will be on lock down without the necklace on."

"That isn't true. The necklace will become a part of you if everything runs smoothly." He said deep in thought.

"Is this part of the plan? Have me controlled?"

"Yes. It was the plan. You had to be controlled, to control those robots. They're still yours. They are floating idly in the air, just waiting for your command." I rolled my eyes in disbelief.

"Don't believe me, see for yourself." Instantly there was a vision of the battle I had just been a part of. I stood foolishly alone, and above my head were my robots. They were just hovering in the air behind me.

It disappeared just as quickly. "Lena." My mother said quickly. I reached for her hand. "I love you." She said rushed and then her hand disappeared from mine.

"Mom?" I said panicked, but my father reached for my hand where my mother's just were.

"Lena there isn't time. Listen to me. Your mother has disappeared, that means I don't have much time to tell you everything I needed to." He said frantic.

"What does this mean? Is this even real?" I asked.

"There isn't any time for that." He said frustrated. "Don't interrupt me while I say this."

"Dad just tell me what to do to defeat them, please." I begged but he held up a hand.

"I can not mess with fate. I can't tell you all the secrets, but I can tell you this. Without control, there is no control."

I rolled my eyes. "Dad that make absolutely no sense at all."

"Listen to me, Lena." He shouted. "You must die for the true antidote to work. You did die. I knew you would die. I knew you would be diseased, cured, and killed. Now you are ready to be reborn. I made it this way so you could fail, without really failing." He was talking fast and desperate, but he continued on.

"There isn't much time, I am fading, I feel it." And he was. His body was starting to disappear. "What shape is your necklace, it is a key shape. The key will set you free from the confines of the necklace. It will be a part of you forever. She knows what to do when the time must come. Lena." He said it all in a blur of a sentence. I saw the light fading. I wanted to call out to him. He was gone. They were *both gone and I was alone again. I was more lost now than I was before.*

I jerked out of the daze. I could see again. There wasn't darkness, but I could not move still. As soon as my eyes focused, I had to blink to make sure I was seeing what I thought I was seeing.

Ahead of me, I saw myself walking. If I could do a double take, I would. Instead, all I could do was watch on. Everyone was engaged in their fights, and did not pay any mind to two Lena's on the battlefield. One frozen in place, and the other walking through the carnage as if nothing was happening at all.

There were dead bodies all around, dead robots, all who would be forgotten. Perhaps Gabe would raise them from the dead to continue his reign. Where was Dr. Ravana? Why wasn't he watching his prisoner?

Suddenly, I watched as the second Lena turned into someone else entirely. He was now a beautiful man. The man I dreamed of so often when I could dream. Square severe jaw, with soft eyes. Jared. Only this Jared had the rot all along his arms. He was sick again.

I wanted to gasp. I wanted to shout. Then without a moment's hesitation, Jared turned into someone I hated. He brought bile to my mouth. The man who tried to take me from his brother, but could not succeed. Aiden.

There was only one explanation for who this was. It was Clementine. She has cloned herself into me while I was under. It didn't hit me when I saw Jared on the battlefield unharmed, when he had just been injected with the disease moments before. Clementine had cloned into not only Jared, but Aiden too. I wanted to scream. I didn't know whose side she was on, and it was killing me not to know.

"Dad." Clem/Aiden called out to Dr. Ravana, and I felt my breath intake. *What was she up to?*

Dr. Ravana turned quickly with a sigh of relief. "Aiden. Thank god. I was so worried about you." He took his left hand, and cupped Aiden's face.

"Here. I'll go destroy the necklace." Clementine said in Aiden's husky voice.

Dr. Ravana smiled in astonishment. "Yes, that would be wise. Do it with any means possible." He turned away as soon as the necklace entered Clementine's hand. Aiden/Clementine walked briskly in my direction, gripping the necklace in her hand.

Before I could even think, Clementine approached me. I wanted to jerk away but I couldn't. She placed the necklace around my neck. When I felt the metal touch my neck, I felt the surge of power. I could move again.

Clementine switched from Aiden back into me and I looked shocked as she took my place, standing still as a statue. She was pretending to be me as I was under control.

The necklace began glowing. I quickly looked to see where Dr. Ravana's attention was, but it was not with me, it was with the battle before us. Clem raised her eyebrows at me in annoyance. "Hide." She whispered quickly.

"What are you doing?" I asked shocked.

"Being you. Go." She said frustrated.

My heart quickened. She was letting me escape. She was on my side.

"Now. Before I change my mind." She whispered heatedly. I didn't hesitate, I ran. I blended in with the fight behind Dr. Ravana, who never knew the Lena behind him, wasn't me at all.

Chapter Twenty: You Can Try
Dr. Ravana

My son was looking at me like he wanted me dead. He was being held by many of my minions. *Yes, I was a batty old man who called them minions.* They remind me of hopeless creatures. They listen without thought. They think in their twisted heads that I have something to offer them. They think they can get something in return for doing my biddings.

My minions were promised a lot, but I would never give it to them. I was sure they knew it deep down. The fact was I had secret weapons all around me. Gabe. Max. Holland. Most of all, Lena. She was the most important weapon to have. Whatever side she was on, was the winning side. I knew that.

I looked back at her. She was really a beautiful girl, even more so now. Her wavy brown hair was blowing in the wind. She was standing like a solider; her arms were by her side, her back straightened in attention. Waiting for a command. I caught sight of her bare neck, and smiled. Her necklace would finally be destroyed. The Antidote, as her father put it. It was laughable. There was no antidote. There was no cure. There was only poison in this world.

I wasn't very protected at the moment. My right hand man, Joseph, was murdered just moments before by Lena. It was a brutal murder, one he truly deserved after what he put Lena through. My other son, Aiden, was off to destroy the necklace that Lena wore all the time. I was out in the open. Anyone who hated me could get me. It was unnerving, but I had my robots to shield me.

His hunch bank and limp step walking towards me made me inhale deeply. Gabe. He finally joined my side. He wasn't much, but he was something. I wasn't alone. They could attack him first.

Before I could even speak to him, a hand wrapped around the back of my neck and whispered softly. "Dr. Ravana." I quickly exhaled when I saw Clementine. My heart pattered at the sight of her. Clementine was so beautiful. She had such dark features, but her eyes always seemed to light up when she smiled at me. Like now, she was beaming serenely at me. I almost forgot that her hand was wrapped around my throat now, in a not so friendly way.

"What's going on?" I asked as her grip tightened. I took a deep gulp of breath.

She playfully squeezed my neck, and released me. "Nothing." She was hiding something. I could feel it.

I peeked around, and panic rose in my throat. "Where is Lena?" I shouted over the clanking of metal that was the fight above us.

Clementine laughed as I looked over in shock. "Calm down. I moved her downstairs. She was just standing there, and they almost pushed her off the building. I swear old man, you never pay attention." My heart warmed at the sound of her voice. Clementine. She made my heart swell.

"Stay safe, my love." I said softly into her ear. She just looked at me hesitantly. She didn't kiss me as she often would. She knew we had to stay secretive, or others would know my weakness. Her.

At that, I heard a crash beside me. I turned to see him on the ground. Jared. My heart took a leap. My son.

No, I stopped myself because I couldn't afford to think this way. We were on different sides of the spectrum. We were two different people. We wanted different things. Love ruled him. Rage ruled me. With us, it was love for the world against rage for the world. It was a fight to the death. It was a fight only one of us could win.

I moved from Clementine's side to Jared's. "Did you think you could truly win, Jared? Did you think this would end with my death or yours? Clearly, I have won already." I hoped my voice didn't crack. I didn't want anyone to see weakness in me.

He didn't respond to my threats. He was a man who was so beaten down now. I hated to see it. He was my son. We weren't weak men.

I heard Gabe rustle behind me, his shoes beating on the ground. Gabe reached Jared, and without a moment's hesitation, he kicked Jared in the side. All that came out of Jared was a moan. I sucked in my breath. Gabe kicked again. This time, Jared let out a howl. He was hurt. This time, I had enough. I sternly shouted. "Gabe. He's mine to finish."

Gabe jerked his head towards me and rolled his eyes, but he backed away quickly, and I felt relief as soon as he stepped away from him.

Jared rolled around on the ground. "We need to kill him while he's down. I will do it." Gabe said simply. He took the gun from his pocket and pointed it to Jared's face.

It was instant. The shot caused a ringing in my ears. Shock. Gabe just shot my son. My son. Yes, we were not on the same page. Yes, we had our differences, but that was my son. Blood began pooling from the wound in his chest. His eyes stared up, unseeing. My son was dead.

Lena came out of nowhere. She fell to the ground at Jared's head. Sobs erupted from her body. Her power was so strong, that the entire ground was shaking in her wake.

He was dead. I knew from her sobs and how powerful they were. He had to be dead. I willed myself to not feel anything. He hated me. I hated him. That was how it was. That was how it would have to stay. Now I had a new dilemma at hand. Lena.

"How is she no longer under control?" I bellowed to Gabe's dumbfounded face. He was fumbling with his device.

"Do something, you useless man." I screamed. He didn't. He just stared ahead, speechless.

"Clementine," I turned to face her again. She was gone. Where had she gone? She hated fights, and confrontation. She probably left the scene as soon as a gun was fired.

I sprang into action since everyone else was hopeless. "Lena." I spoke through the sound of metals clanking, and crushing sounds. "I command you to stop."

That was when she raised her head to meet mine. She was going to kill me. I could feel the rage all over her body. I was still a part of her. I was still capable of controlling her someway or another. I had to be.

"I am here to kill you. I have nothing to lose, *Master.*" She said the last words as if they were venom on her tongue.

"Gabe." I bawled again. He stared at the magnificence of her. The sheer marvelousness of a girl who broke control one too many times.

"I think Gabe is too tongue tied to help you out." She spoke as if she were hissing now.

"As your master, I command you to stay." I tried once more. She laughed her villainous laugh.

"Did you really think that would work?" she laughed bitterly. "I think your time is up."

"Don't you want to know the secret of how you keep breaking the spell every time?" I tried.

This got her attention. She stopped moving towards me, and looked deep in thought. "I don't want anything from you. The truth is a lie when it comes out of your mouth." She jumped up into the air, and landed right in front of my face. "I think I have had enough of you altogether."

She raised her hand and slammed it down onto my head. I fell instantly. I was an old man, after all, and I had no fight in me. I couldn't take her on. She knew it. I knew it.

I was on the ground, holding my head. I thought I was seeing stars. She kneeled down to my eye level. She was smiling viciously. She was just getting started. I heard a smack, and cringed at the sound. It was a dreadful sound. A sound I never wanted to here again. Her smile began to fade until the light seemed to go out of her eyes.

Her villainous smile was gone now. Her eyes were dimming. A knife was sticking out of her arm. Deep into where the cure or the robotic insertion was placed in Lena. I looked to see who stabbed her.

Gabe stood triumphal beside her. A stab to the cure's central area killed them if a gunshot wound to the head would not. I hadn't told him, but he figured it out. H didn't stop there. Gabe brought the knife down into her head. Her heart. Her neck. He was a butcher, a mad man, and a villain to the core.

Lena stumbled back until she was beside Jared. She collapsed down until her hand was touching his. She was struggling to breathe. She couldn't be saved. Even her abilities couldn't heal her wounds because of the damage to the central cure area.

The fatal wound to her arm would never heal. Lena's robotic abilities were destroyed when Gabe stabbed and destroyed her central line to being a robot. The cure was ruined in Lena forever.

They lay together. Two despaired souls who depended too much on love. The sight was unbearable for me. Love had killed them. Love had shattered me so many years ago, I knew love was useless, but they had not learned that yet.

"You killed our main source, Gabe. You gave our biggest secret away as well. Now they will know how to defeat the robots." I growled to Gabe.

"Who? Who is left? Our last "defenders of the world," are dead on the floor." He said sarcastically, using air quotes and all, which I hated.

There was still clinging in the air, none of them caring of the destruction happening on the ground. By the looks of it, as Lena's breathe became even quieter, her robots stopped their fights. She was truly fading away.

She gripped her necklace in her hands. I froze. She was going to do something with that necklace. Did she somehow have another trick up her sleeve? I watched with eagerness. What was she capable of in her final moments? It was fascinating.

Instead she took the necklace from her neck. The necklace was the only thing keeping her alive. I knew there were unknown powers within the necklace. Lena couldn't be controlled for long because of that thing. I knew it. I knew Sebastian well. He gave her that necklace. I watched him do it before I killed him on Lena's dance recital day. It was a secret I never told anyone.

I almost changed my mind that very day, but I had too much at stake. Sebastian was getting in the way. They all were.

She didn't hesitate in her movements. She was already struggling to breathe without the necklace. Her father had done great work with it. He kept her alive when she should have been dead for some time now. I should have saw it coming. I should have known what she planned to do next. She placed the necklace around Jared's neck. As soon as the necklace left her body, blood began to pour from her mouth.

It was marvelous to see. He took a deep breath in, while her breath grew shallow until there were none. She was gone.

Love. Love. Love. His new breaths seem to shout at me. She died for love, and he was reborn from love.

Chapter Twenty-One: Say Goodbye Jared

As soon as the necklace went around my neck, I felt a jolt. The healing powers that the necklace possessed began to restore me instantly. The gunshot wound closed, but not before spitting the bullet out for me. I was myself again. I felt a new drive within me at that moment.

Energy, fury, rage flowed through me. I felt invincible. I felt power. I felt everything Lena felt. *Felt*.

My girlfriend, my love, was dead. I knew she was gone because I could see everything she saw. My lifeless body on the ground. Gabe stabbing Lena, destroying the cure that was inside her. All her robotic parts were destroyed inside of her. She felt the tear from herself. However, the robotic abilities seemed to be memorized in the necklace because I felt powers inside of me that I never knew I could possess.

He revealed how to stop the robots without meaning to. That was Gabe though, careless and stupid. And now I would kill my friend. I would kill Gabe. I would kill them all.

Gabe was standing with his mouth open and staring dumbly into my eyes. He was shocked, and Holland beside him was smiling at me. I frowned at her.

There were no words that needed to be spoken, I gripped Gabe by the front of his shirt and thrust him in the air, before slamming us both back down into the ground. He landed with a smack on the ground.

"First you try to kill me, and then you kill Lena. Do you really think you will be the last one standing now?" Gabe tried to pick himself off the ground, but I was faster. I punched him in the gut. It was a powerful punch. He started to spit out the blood gathering in his mouth.

His hands were up in an instance. Swarms of robots gathered around me. I jumped in the air to become eye level with them. I was amazed that I was right. Lena's necklace seemed to encompass all her powers inside of it. I had Lena's powers now. We were one.

I held my hands out in front of me as I had seen Lena do so many times. I screamed in anger as one of the robots threw a ball of light at me that burned like a bitch.

I dodged the next ball, and to my astonishment. I saw red hair. Clown red hair. With a burnt scalp. I stopped.

She tried everything she could to never become a robot, and here she was. She was not a nice person, but no one deserved this fate. Kaley. Lena's ex best friend. The girl that tried countless times to kill Lena, and didn't succeed. Now I would have to kill her because Gabe had thrown her in my path. I didn't want her. I wanted my father and Gabe to suffer and hurt. I didn't want to wound any of them.

That was when she launched forward towards me. Her eyes as red as her hair. She reached me but I was faster.

As my screams filled the air, so did my energy. Without a moment's hesitation, all the robots moved away from me as the blast rocketed towards them. Kaley was blown into obliteration, while some just moved out of my way. They fell to the sea, and some to the building with a crash.

I flew down and grabbed Gabe by the neck. "Jared, please." He cried out, but I wasn't through with him. I ignored his cries. He was too far-gone. He was a monster. He didn't feel anything.

"Jared." Another voice called out. I saw my father walking towards me. I dropped Gabe to the building. He landed sprawled out, not dead, but hurt.

My father stood with pride as he always had. Controlled, poised, never faltering in his stance. He looked sincere almost with the simple way he said my name.

"Jared, this isn't about you. None of this is. Stay out of our way. We are almost done. There is only you who stands in our way of whole world domination. Lena is dead. Everyone is under mind control. What are you still fighting for? Who do you have to fight for anymore? You don't." his speech felt endless. He was right, of course, but I couldn't let them win without a fight.

I was so lost in his speech, that I lost sight of where Gabe was. He had moved from his crouched position, leading a trail of blood to where Holland had been standing.

Now Holland had a gun pressed against Gabe's chest, and she was looking at him intently.

"Holland?" I asked in awe.

"Hush, I am busy." She said simply.

"What is going on?" I asked. I turned back to Dr. Ravana who was watching in wonderment.

"I am on your side, Jared. I can't believe you doubted me this much." I couldn't see Gabe's face, but I knew the betrayal would be apparent in his face.

"Love doesn't always win then." My father whispered slowly.

"Love does win." I said simply back. "Love for friends can win sometimes too." I shrugged my shoulders.

Holland continued. "Gabe says the control system is under the island. Do you know anything about that? Blow up the system. Blow up the mind control central area. The robots will be humans again. Can you handle that?" she asked me.

She pulled out a second gun, and pointed it to my father, who threw his hands up in surrender.

I could handle that. I could handle anything because I had Holland back.

Chapter Twenty-Two: A Shot in Hell
Jared

Holland still had the gun to Gabe, and the other gun on my father. They both looked defeated. I peered down at Lena's lifeless body. I had lost her so many times, but never this clearly.

I took the necklace from my neck and threw it around Lena's neck as she had done for me. I waited. I willed her to take a breath. "Please." I whispered to her.

Nothing happened. She had already bled out onto the ground. She was blue. She was cold. "Please." I cried again. "Don't leave me yet." The robots above had stopped fighting, and watched below.

It was over.

"Let me through." A soft voice spoke through the silence. I heard audible gasps from behind me.

"Clem? No. Clementine" my dad's voice cracked as he spoke in shock. I jerked my head over. She was back. It was the girl who cloned herself as me, and then Lena. She had her black hair, and apparently her name was Clementine. My father was traumatized; I could only guess there was a long story there. As she approached, I threw my body over Lena's.

"Get away." I shouted to her. "Please. Just let her be." My heart was breaking, but I couldn't do anything about it.

"Let me help her." She said simply.

I heard my father suck in his breath, as his face turned from awe to betrayal.

"Jared." She touched my shoulder and my heart began beating faster. Familiar. Soft. She felt like someone I knew. I looked into her eyes. She nodded to me as if to tell me everything would be just fine. It felt as if I was being hypnotized by her very look. In that moment, I realized that I had never trusted someone so much before, as I trusted her right now.

I moved to the side, and gave her room to kneel beside Lena. I didn't know what she planned to do, but whatever it was, I knew that she wouldn't harm Lena.

She slipped the necklace off her neck and I reached my hand out to grab her. *Oh no. Lena definitely wouldn't survive without the necklace.*

I reached my hands out once more to grab the necklace form her hands, but Clementine shot a hand out in front of my face.

I tried to move again, but it finally occurred to me that Clementine had me frozen in this position. All I could do was watch the scene unfold before me.

Clementine took the necklace, and slammed it into the ground. I wanted to break my trance, and hit her for destroying the necklace, but she didn't stop her beating of the necklace against the ground.

When she was satisfied, she took the key and raised it above her head. She took in a collected breath, and looked over to me. Before I could interpret what was happening, she slammed with all her might down into Lena's heart.

The sound coming from Lena could only be described as a horror movie cry. She was awake and that was all that mattered to me.

To my surprise, I could feel again. I could move; I could smile. My face wouldn't stop smiling when I saw Lena's bright eyes open up to me. Hazel, never to be red again. Clementine released me from my frozen trance. I took the moment of freedom and grabbed Lena's hand. Her scream had died down.

Warmth begins to spread through her body. I feel her hand become clammy with heat and sweat. She was alive once more. All stabs wounds were healed.

"What did you do?" I asked in admiration to Clementine.

"I gave her the true cure." She stood quickly.

"The what?" I shouted.

She ignored me and continued, "Jared. The robots won't be robots any longer if they have no one to lead them. Destroy every leader here." She said it as if it were the simplest thing in the world. She grabbed my cheek and I felt that weird warmth again. "Jared." She spoke my name as if it were a sermon. "You did well. You did so well."

At that, she took flight into the air, leaving me stunned. "Robots. Listen to me." Every head jerked towards her. "The control system in the bottom of the ocean is your main control source. Let's destroy it. I have the cure in my hands." She showed Lena's necklace to all that could see it. "If I can jam this into the computer brain. It will explode. It won't be able to revive itself because this necklace contains the antidote. The antidote to cruelty. The end to all ends. While you still have your powers. Escape. Leave." This was her final word. She turned without another peep.

I ran to watch her over the edge of the building. She dived into the water, and she was on her way to the hidden control room under the island. She was going to blow up everything that stood on this island.

Everyone was flying away. Lena's eyes met mine in a wide-eyed gaze. She levitated into the air, amused. She still had her powers. *But how?* She jerked my hand up, and we grabbed Dr. Ravana from his staggered stance. Holland grabbed Gabe, still holding the gun against him. I jerked Holland up and flew them off the island. I still had Lena's powers somehow as well.

When we reached the island that Holland and I had once been on, the sound was deafening. The exposition was huge, and I could feel the warmth upon my face even though we were miles apart from the island.

Debris reached us even from the distance as well. The compound was destroyed. It was up in flames. There was no way that Clementine made it out alive. She was dead. She sacrificed it all for the greater good.

My father dropped to his knees before my eyes, looking at his masterpiece; destroyed. The former robots were looking all around in confusion. Eyes no longer glowing. Some ran for each other, hugging and kissing. Lena watched in joy at the sight of them.

"It looks like it's over." My father was on the ground beside me. He wasn't looking at me. It was as if I hadn't even spoken.

His lips were moving, but I couldn't make out the words, so I walked closer to him. He was muttering over and over. "Clem. Clementine." Shocked, I looked at his face. His eyes were filled with tears.

I jerked my head towards the island that was up in flames. *Clementine? Why did Clementine matter to him at all?*

I ignored him, and found Holland was in awe looking at the flames. I could finally breathe again knowing she was on my side, and would never turn her back on me. I was thanking my lucky stars that we both made it out alive.

That was when I saw something in the shadows of the trees. I held my breath as Aiden came around the corner. He was definite in his steps. He walked with a purpose. He was here to destroy something. *Who helped him off the island anyways? I had hoped he was there when the explosion happened.*

Holland heard him quick enough and turned the gun off of Gabe to point it at Aiden. It was fast. The whole thing. One moment, Holland was in control of the gun, and then she wasn't.

Gabe jerked the gun out of Holland's hand. He tricked her for the last time. He turned the gun on Aiden.

"Don't make another move." Gabe shouted. My heart sped up. *Did this mean he was on our side?* Aiden threw up his hands in surrender, but he kept walking forward towards us.

"Gabe, you might want to drop the gun away from me, before you lose everything."

"Everything." Gabe laughed. "What do I have? The girl I love doesn't love me back." Holland turned sharply to Gabe. She did love him. How could he still not know? "My friends have all turned their backs on me." I wanted to laugh at that one, but I let the disaster unfold before me. "I have nothing to lose." Gabe said through gritted teeth.

"I can think of one." He didn't elaborate further, but he continued his speech. "We have lost everything, because of you. Lena was able to return with your silly mistake of showing them how to counteract the cure. You have ruined everything. It is not forgiven. By me, by my father, by anyone who died in vain." His voice was rising, and his face was turning almost purple from his fury.

"Aiden, I did nothing." Gabe simply answered.

"You did everything. You did everything wrong. Now, you must suffer for it." Aiden was through talking. He reached around him and pointed the gun he had been carrying at Gabe.

Gabe looked unfazed by the sight of the gun. He wasn't afraid to die. His eyes even begged Aiden to shoot him down. That was when Aiden turned the gun to Holland. That got Gabe's attention. He threw his body in front of hers, but it was too late. Aiden pulled the trigger. I would never forget the sound of that gunshot firing.

Gabe making a futile attempt to save Holland. The sound of Holland gasping. Lena gripping me shirt. The bullet hitting Holland right in the chest as she fell to the ground.

My heart stopped. It was that fast. One moment, I had my best friend back, and in the next moment, she was dying.

Gabe was on the floor before anyone else. Surprising me, and everyone else. Lena had her hand to her mouth, holding in a sob. My father looked on in amazement.

Aiden just smiled victoriously. "Looks like you did have something to lose." Aiden chanted over and over again.

Gabe was not paying attention. He was holding Holland in his hands. He looked down at her.

She was trying to speak, but all that came out were muffled, gargling sounds. My heart was breaking at the scene. He looked deep into her eyes, and said the words he couldn't say before this moment. "I love you, Holland. I hope you never doubted it, even for a minute."

I knew those muffled sounds were her trying to say them back. Gabe did too. He kept saying, "I know, I know." And then his sobs grew louder. And I knew she was gone.

I didn't even get to say goodbye, or that I was sorry for the things I had said. Or the fact that I had doubted her loyalty to me.

Gabe didn't waste any time. He placed Holland's head gently on the ground. And then his eyes met mine. There were words we needed to say, had to say, but we couldn't say them now. Our best friend was dead, and she needed some avenging. Now.

Gabe faced the gun towards Aiden. I felt my blood pumping. He would be dead. Finally. The gun clicked uselessly in Gabe's hand. Empty. The gun was out of bullets. Aiden was at an advantage. He viciously laughed, while pointing the gun at Gabe's face.

Chapter Twenty-Three: The Big Guns
Jared

I never thought I would see the day when I would agree with Gabe again, but the time had come. We were both furious. I could feel Lena fuming beside me too.

She already hated Aiden with a passion. He was one of the people who turned her into a mindless robot. He was one of her worst nightmares. Her worst enemy too.

Holland was dead on the ground. Her lifeless body was fueling my anger. There was no necklace to cure her. There was nothing to bring her back. She was forever lost, and my heart couldn't handle it. Before I could even think about it, Gabe was tackling Aiden to the ground.

There was only one gun between them that worked, and Gabe was going in for the kill. He wanted the gun. Aiden had taken the one thing he loved from him.

Aiden was at the advantage. He was faster, stronger, more coordinated than Gabe would ever dream of being. Gabe's powers seemed to truly die with the explosion. His eyes were no longer red either. Aiden had the gun pressed to Gabe's forehead when my father's voice broke through the commotion.

"Don't kill him." My father pleaded to Aiden.

Aiden turned quick to look at my father. The barrel still pushed to Gabe. There was hatred and venom in his eyes.

"This is all your fault. This is all you. You have destroyed everything." Aiden screamed. Shrieked even. I had never seen him so angry.

"I will kill everyone standing here. We lost, old man. You promised us eternal greatness. And now look how far we have fallen."

My father looked on in amusement. "You would never get any of that. You would never receive the things you so strove to get."

With that, Gabe punched Aiden in the jaw, causing Aiden to drop the gun. Gabe was fast. He took the gun in his hands and pulled the trigger. Gabe was never a good shot, so it was no surprise when the bullet missed Aiden's forehead, but instead grazed the side of his face.

Aiden shouted in pain, cursing my father the entire way.

"Now I have been shot because of you. How much more must I go through?" Aiden grunted. He reminded me of a child crying over spilled milk.

"There comes a time, Aiden, when you have to take blame for the things you have done. There comes a time when those more powerful than you finally win." My father didn't elaborate. That was what my father did best. He spoke in circles that no one could keep up with it.

"Father. Enough." Aiden screamed harshly at him. My father stayed stoic.

"Aiden. It is over. Give up already."

"Give up. Oh, give up?" Aiden was going mad. "I will never give up. I won't give up until my last breath."

"That is what is wrong with the world. It is why I tried to change things."

"Change things? By what? Forcing people to follow you. You pathetic, old man." He spat at his feet. Lena held her breath beside me. Her chest stopped moving against mine. He had been in her head for months. She knew what would piss him off. This was one of those things that would anger him.

"Corruption. Men like you. Angry at the world. Blaming everyone but yourself. You are the root of all evil. They say money is, and yes money is evil, but not as evil as mankind. I am the bad guy because I tried to overturn that evil. I stand by what I did. Nothing can change the world, except love. I see that now." I was in awe at his words. He always captivated anyone who listened. He talked in riddles. He was mad, but you could never forget that he was a genius too.

"Can you just stop talking, father?" Aiden was cringing at my father's words.

"Maybe you should remember how weak you are right now? Without any weapons." Gabe finally pointed out to him.

"You hide behind your robots. You hide behind my father. You are nothing without that mind control. Your control died with that island back there. What are you without it?" Aiden shouted to them both. Gabe's face said it all that Aiden was right.

"Then I have nothing to lose right?" Gabe pulled the trigger. As soon as the bullet went off, missing Aiden completely. There was crash as Gabe toppled on his back.

He landed right beside Holland. It was almost symbolic. They were together. Soon to be two bloody corpses, instead of one.

The dagger was sticking out of Gabe's chest, where Aiden had just hit him square on. He gagged on the ground, reaching for Holland. Aiden stepped forward, jerking the blade from his chest, causing Gabe to sputter blood. Aiden took the gun from his pale hands.

My father cried out at the sight. "Aiden, please."

"Yes, father. Beg for me to stop. This is your entire fault. Every last death is your fault. You're next." It was a bloody massacre on this island. No one could stop it. The villains were killing one another in front of our eyes. The blood was off our hands.

"Kill me then. I couldn't change anyone. I made the mistake of letting crooked men in on the plan." My father shouted.

Aiden didn't hesitate. The shot rang through the air. I wasn't sure where my father was hit, and I didn't care. He was my father.

I dropped to my knees beside him as soon as he landed. Lena grabbing my shoulder to stop me but I couldn't be stopped, even if I wanted to be.

I reached my hand to hold his cheek. Aiden made a sound behind me, and for a moment I thought he would come after me. The weight on my shoulder lifted.

There was a sound of a crack. Lena hit Aiden one more time. His arm was completely broken. The bone was sticking out of his skin, and the gun lay on the ground beside them. Lena jerked it up and faced Aiden. "Don't you ever try to kill my boyfriend again," she was furious. Aiden had tried to take me out when my back was turned. "Take him away." Lena commanded, as a mass of people surrounded Aiden.

"Jared." My father moaned. "Please. Know how much I loved you. Your mother. Jared, I did this all for you." My father was delusional. He was. He hadn't told me he loved me in years. I might have even loved him deep down.

"Jared." He reached for my hand. I let him.

"There is something you must know. Please." His voice was fading.

"What is it?" I whispered to him. I squeezed his hands. "Father?" I called out to him, but his breaths were shallow.

I was losing him. I was losing him before he could tell me his truths. His faults.

"Father?" I put my head against his chest. His breaths were no longer. He was gone. I would never know what he had to say to me.

I didn't sob. Even though my heart should have felt empty when it came to him, I still loved my father. He had done such wrong to the world, but it didn't matter at the moment. Death was everywhere, and I couldn't stop it. I had lost three people in a matter of minutes.

I turned slowly as Gabe heaved on the ground. He kept repeating my name over and over. It was crazy how the people who betrayed me, needed me as they died. They didn't deserve me, but I wouldn't turn my back on them as they had done to me. I reached him on the ground. "Jared. Please. Forgive me. Holland."

I didn't truly mean it yet, but I would give him peace in his final moments. "I forgive you, Gabe." Perhaps one day I would truly mean it. His eyes shut at the sound. A serene look passed his face. He was gone.

There was hissing coming from the ground and I turned to find Aiden struggling for breath. He killed Holland, my father and Gabe. Yes, two of them were almost dead to me before, but they were a part of me all the same.

"Jared, help me." Aiden whispered. Last one to call out for me in their deaths. He was being held up by a girl I didn't recognize, but by the look on her face, I knew that my brother had used her in one way or another when she was under control. Lena watched with pride in her eyes. She wanted Aiden hurt too. I didn't blame her.

His face was pure terror. It was strange to see it on his face. He was my brother. I wanted to help. But then I remembered he killed my father without a second thought. He killed Gabe without another blink. Anyone who I ever loved was gone and taken from me by Aiden.

The former robots were circling him. They were vicious. They were unforgiving. They would rip him apart for what he did to them.

"Take him away." I said simply. His eyes widened at the sound. He deserved it. After all, he was a wicked man.

Chapter Twenty- Four: The Power You Keep

"Is it really over?"

"It's really over."

"I can't believe they're all gone. We are one of the only people left standing." I said.

"That is true, but look around you." I did. "Look at all the people we saved. Look at all those people that were robots just an hour ago. You did that." She was beaming at me.

"No, kid. We did that." I brought my lips down to hers. My heart swelled. She was my Lena. She would never be another Lena. She would never be controlled. She would live out her days in full control of who she was. She had herself to thank for that.

"Look what I can still do though." She said as we broke our kiss. She lifted herself easily into the air.

"I know. I am still unsure how you can do that after Clementine blew up the control center." I said in awe.

"Clementine. She was a mystery, but she sacrificed it all to end this war." She looked wary, but changed the subject. "Try it yourself. Try to levitate. I saw you grab Holland and fly away with me off the roof." She smiled down at me. I didn't know what to do.

"Eh. What do I do?" I asked unsure.

"Well, how did you do it before?" she giggled.

"I was angry. I didn't even think about it."

"Exactly. Don't think, just do. Just imagine yourself in the air, and will yourself to do it. Very simple." She laughed at me as I jumped pathetically.

"No. Just think, and it will happen. Promise. Just close your eyes and concentrate." She smiled that big grin at me and I closed my eyes.

Moments passed, and neither of us said a word. "Are you ever going to open your eyes?" She snickered. I peered one eye open and to my surprise, I was right beside her. I looked down only to see the trees below us.

"See. I told you."

"What is this? Why do we still have powers? I thought that died when the compound was destroyed." I repeated. I was rambling, and she shook her head. "I don't know how or why. I am not going to question it. I am just going with it." She beamed at me.

"I guess Gabe and my father didn't think that through."

"No, they thought it through. They just never thought that they would be defeated." She wisely told me.

"I wonder what he was trying to tell me there in the end." I would never know what my father had been dying to tell me. I would never know what the last words were on his lips, and why they were meant for me to interpret and no one else.

"I don't know. Maybe he was getting in one last insult." I said as I shrugged.

"I don't think so." Lena spoke after a moment of hesitation. "I think he wanted to tell his son goodbye before it was too late." I shook my head, but she continued. "Yes, he was an awful man but near the end there, I thought he was going to change his ways."

"You're right though. He was acting so strange all night. What was the deal about love, and Clementine? I will never understand."

"Maybe we weren't meant to always understand. Maybe we were just meant to live and be happy."

"You sound so zen right now." I laughed at her and she laughed back. The sound was glorious. I never thought I would hear our happiness again. I never thought I would stand beside her and not be her enemy. I was her equal again.

"What now?" she asked.

"We live. We live out the rest of our days together."

Then I had a thought. I knew exactly what I wanted to do.

"Lena?" I asked bashfully. "I know everyone we love is dead. I know everything in the world is a little shaky. We are all we have. Truthfully, you are all I need or want. We are standing beside the dead, but I want us to live. Each day of our lives together. I know this is an awful time." I got down on one of my knees, to her shock, and my own. "I know that, but would you do me the honor of marrying me?"

She was staring at me with her mouth agar. *Shit, this was a terrible idea.*

She didn't speak for what felt like an eternity. "Well, where is my ring, Jared?" she broke out in a fit of laughs and my nerves slipped away.

"When there is a shop open for rings again. I will get you the biggest ring I can find." I kissed her knuckles. And she got down on her knees in front of me so that we were eye level.

"Of course I will marry you. Hell, the world is practically under. Should we even have to have an official marriage?" She asked seriously.

"Hmm, I want it in writing." Her eyes lit up at the sound.

"I love you, Jared."

"I love you too, fiancé."

She snickered, and the sound was music to my ears. I could die a happy man listening to the very sound.

Epilogue:
12 years later

"Mom." Lily shouted into the air repeatedly. I frantically ran to the backyard. My heart speeding up with each step I took.

"What is it, Lily?" I shouted as I reached her. She had both hands in the air. She was facing the flowers in the garden. They had just died two days before. The pollution in the air made it hard for things to grow anymore.

It was hard for the earth to recover from such destruction. Dr. Ravana, and his followers had caused the world to lose a lot, because we were now under populated, and everything that grew, died days later. We made it work though. We had to, to survive.

"Where's dad? He has to see this too." She shouted over her shoulder to me.

"He isn't home, baby." I smiled and kneeled beside her. "You're doing it." I squealed. She smiled back at me as she raised her hands higher.

The flowers started to bloom before my very eyes. "Oh honey. They're beautiful." She could make anything dead grow once more. Her powers were very subtle before, but now they were growing more intensely. Her powers were finally in. I often wondered if her power could apply to humans, but was too afraid to try the theory out.

"Where is Noah?" she asked in a hurry.

"Hold that thought." I got up quickly and ran into the house. "Noah. Your sister wants to show you something." When he didn't answer. I hurried down to his room. We lived in my old house. It was one of the only houses still standing all those years ago. We redecorated, rebuilt, and made a family here.

My father's lab was now Noah's lab. He got the genius gene from my father. I was so glad. He was so smart. I saw parts of my father reflected in Noah everyday.

"Noah?" I asked. I knocked on his lab door. The door was locked, so I beat on it once more. Mid knock, Noah opened the door. "What did I say about locking the lab door? If something were to go wrong, who could get to you?"

He ignored me and continued, "Mom. I can't be disturbed. I am having a breakthrough. Right now."

I rolled my eyes. He was having a breakthrough every few hours, if we were being honest. "Honey, your sister is making the flowers grow. Her powers are coming in. I know you remember how excited you were when your powers came in." I added. He didn't so much as smile at that.

The world was very different now. When Clementine blew up the control system, and there was no longer mind control, the people who were once robots, including myself, retained many powers. I passed them down to my children. The world now had many problems, but along with that there were many superhuman running around. Thanks Dr. Ravana.

"Come down, now. Show me what you're working on later." He finally sighed and turned to me. He slammed the lab door shut behind me, and locked it.

I held my hand out to him, and he took it. We ran down the steps and into the backyard. He was turned with his back to me. I felt the butterflies all over. He was home.

"Daddy!" Noah yelled, releasing my hand, and reaching his father in an instant. Super speed. Noah had super speed. It came in handy when he was working on his science projects.

Jared picked Noah up into a bear hug. He kissed his forehead, and took two strides forward to reach me. He kissed me while the children yelled "ewwww."

"How are you, my love?" he murmured.

"Great, now that you're here." I whispered. "Look what Lily is doing." I pointed to her, and his face lit up instantly with satisfaction.

"Lily! You've got the flowers to grow. Look at that." He said cheerfully, causing Lily to squeal in delight.

She smiled and finally released her hands. "I'll have to come back and check them to make sure they don't die on me. Just think how much I could save." She was delighted with herself. Jared rustled her hair.

Noah clapped his hands together. "My turn!" he took off running into the house and we tagged along after him.

"Tada." He said as we entered the lab.

"What is it, buddy?" Jared said with a smile.

He pointed to the rabbit on his desk. "This morning, this rabbit had cancer in his eye, but after I injected him with medicine, that I created, he is all better." I felt my smile freeze on my face. My heart was pattering loudly. I could hear Jared's heart beating faster too. Noah continued.

"I have discovered the cure for all diseases. Cancer included." My heart did a little tumble. I felt my face sinking. Jared simply smiled, but I could feel the tense air in the room.

"Son, I couldn't be more proud of you. I think it is time though. We have something to tell you. About why the world is the way it is now." Jared said softly.

Lily raised her hands. "Oh, oh. Let me tell him." She laughed her little giggle. She didn't know anything. It seemed that she was too young to know such things.

"Jared, take Lily downstairs. I'll be there soon." He nodded, and guided Lily out of the room as she shouted she wanted to hear the news.

"Noah, let's sit."

***

After I finished telling Noah everything, and I mean everything that transpired, he understood why this could end badly. He just wanted to help people. I told him that he would. He would do it the right way, but I told him to trust very few on his endeavor.

I left Noah to his lab, to his project to save the world. He would save it the right way as he vowed to me. He promised to perfect the medicine he created, and that he would share it with no one, and that money would not drive his experiment.

As soon as I entered the kitchen, my heart felt content. Jared was there. His arms were crossed, as he leaned against the counter, just waiting for me. He was my rock. He made me steady in this very unsteady world. "Well, crisis averted." I smiled and kissed Jared's cheek, but he was distracted.

"I heard the whole thing. You did wonderful, Lena. Lily is outside attempting to grow the bushes back now." He said, but his attention was distracted.

"What's wrong? You seem a little stressed." I asked.

"I found this in the mail." Jared held out an envelope to me. There was no return address, but instead read, "open when you're ready."

"Ready for what?" I asked curiously.

"I have no idea." Jared was shaking his head in confusion.

He opened the envelope with one swift movement. At the sight, he dropped the envelope.

"What? What is it?" I panicked, as he pointed to the letter. I picked it up.

Inside was my necklace, burnt to a pulp, but still there, and two scraps of paper. I felt like I couldn't breath. I was happy to see my necklace. It represented my family, but still. I couldn't shake the uneasiness I felt.

"Clementine?" I felt chills all over. She was the last person to have my necklace. It had to be her.

"I don't know." He regained his composure, and opened the tiny letter first.

Dear Jared and Lena,
The past is behind us, but first, here is a little inside to your father, Jared. He loved you, and I loved him. The truth is I love you too. You may never understand this, and this may not be closure, but we must see our mistakes to prevent them from happening again. I am long gone now. I hope this arrives when I planned, but sometimes our plans fall through. I'm sorry for cloning the both of you. I'm sorry for a lot of things. Jared, I want you to know how much I love you. Although I will die as Clementine, my name is Chelsea Ravana. Jared, my son, I had to hide. I had to watch your father. I had to make this right. I am sorry I left you, but you know I was always with you. Your father wrote this to me when Lena first came to the compound. He never knew the truth of who I was, but he still loved Clementine. I guess love never dies. You know this firsthand. Lena, take care of my son.
Goodbye, I love you forever.
C

We sat there in awe. He didn't speak for a long time. I was in shock, but I had to be a wife. I had to be a friend, an equal. I had to pull us through it.

I kissed his cheek. "Well, the worst is over right?" I smiled.

He looked me over. "Wow. I can't believe it." He looked as if he would pass out from the news.

"I know. Should we keep reading?" I rubbed his cheek. He had to snap out of it.

"Yes. Even if it gets worse. You're here, and I love you. We will get through anything." He smiled at me and I held his hand as we opened the second letter.

"Together?" he whispered.

"Forever."

THE END

The Lost Letter

October 7, 2031

Dear My Love,

I didn't write your name in case someone finds this. I have a few confessions. I have a few regrets. I figured I would start with this.

Sometimes I really wished Jared were on my side, instead of Aiden. I know what you're thinking, *why would you want someone who hates you on your side? Why does it matter?*

The truth is, I loved Jared. No, I love Jared. I loved their mother. I loved all of humanity. But then I saw the world as it truly was. The world was obsessed with things it shouldn't have been. It was obsessed with money.

In a world driven by money and power, one can only survive by playing the same game. I was going to destroy the earth and leave them floundering without their money. Drown without their power because I would be their leader.

The world doesn't need saving, the world needs retribution, and I will be the one to give it to them. Justice. I am serving justice. I am performing my civic duty, and destroying the world for what it has become. Can you understand that?

Humanity has been lost for a long time. There is not one kind person left, or so it seems. There is not one person who hasn't been corrupted by sex, lust, money or power. I am not excluding myself, but I am going to get rid of it all before it is too late.

Do you understand my purpose? Do you understand the duty that I have to finish it all?

If you look around, there is truly no one there who will take the time of day to care about you. In a world without compassion, there is nothing. The world today is cold. We stare blankly at the homeless man on the side of the road; we stare unfeeling at the woman selling her body on the streets to pay for her children. We turn a blank eye to all the world's problems.

That was where it began. Sebastian wanted to protect the human race. There was nothing we would get in return. When I asked if we could help the poor, he didn't have an answer. That was when I realized he was driven by money as well. That day I went home, kissed my wife goodnight. I decided that night that I wouldn't stand by money. I would destroy the disease that was meant to help all people. It truly meant he and I would only help the rich.

I know it's cruel, to kill so many and to make them under my control but I am playing the game of life. I am the ideal example of fear. Now that I have created fear, money isn't of importance. Nothing is important any longer but the fear in the hearts of everyone. I have controlled Sebastian's daughter who I have meant to control since day one. The problem is that Jared fell in love.

The truth is, I wanted to have Jared on my side but then he fell in love. He fell in love with my enemy. I couldn't believe it when I knew and I felt shattered. Aiden had followed me no matter what. I wanted Jared to do that as well, and he didn't. He blamed me for their mother's death as I blamed him when I was angry. I caused Aiden to turn on him too and I don't regret it but I wish I didn't have to kill Jared, as I have to kill Lena.

Love is the one thing that can break someone, destroy their thoughts, their feelings and anything rational about them. Love broke me when I fell in love. Love broke me when I loved my sons. Love broke me when I found out my friend was like the rest of them. Love breaks us all. I set out to destroy love from the world and I have succeeded.

Gabe and Holland were once in love and then I gave Gabe power. It completes my theory how power thirst is more important than love. Power and money destroyed a love that seemed to hold a lifetime of promise.

A man turned his back on the one who loved him to be a ruler and it proves to me once more that what I am doing is right. I am murdering society's ways. I am murdering the vile of the world.

Jared is foolish to not be with me but I won't ever let him know that I love him. I think of him everyday. I think of how if the world were different, I could pat him on the back for finding a girl who loved him. I couldn't let them be destroyed by society though.

If this world were the same as it once was, they would become bored with one another. Cheat, lie and lie some more. Love fails. For many reasons. But now their love won't fail, it will live with them in death.

They will die at the prime of their romance before they could destroy one another. They should be thanking me. Power is above love, and one day he might have found power more thrilling than love.

He is broken, from the love he feels for this girl. It broke my heart inside to know that Lena would never be the girl he fell in love with after I was through with her. She would be a solider in my army.

Gabe is being punished now for his once love for Holland, but in all honesty, he is one of the most malicious people I have ever encountered.

I will put an end to this. The people that are like Gabe are the worst kind and the reason why I do this. I want to keep people safe from this by taking them out of the situation.

I can see Jared now. I know his every move. I know everything about the world because I am the sole owner now. I love Jared but I have to destroy him. He fights for the ones that are evil.

I wanted to let him think he was still winning. Let him think that I didn't know the truth. One day I hope he knows the truth about me. I love him. I even love Lena but I can't have this anymore. Please tell Jared for me if I am dead before I can. And if he doesn't force me to kill him anyways.

I just need to see one act of kindness and genuine compassion to break what I have built up. To change my view of humanity. I have waited for years to see it one true act of love, and I still haven't.

This may be our last letter. There won't be much time for letters after this. I know Jared will come after me. I know he will kill me. I know what comes for me and I am ready to leave the world in destruction. No one could rebuild it but Lena, and look where she is now.

I want to leave the world in obliteration. I want the world to never remember what once was. I want them to remember what is left when I am finished. I don't care if it's possible for them to find their way in the dark. I don't care if anyone ever forgives me for what I have done. I don't want it. I want the world to be renewed. I want the world to be rejuvenated.

Is it possible? Is it possible to recreate a world that is so damaged?

Bigger and better is the concept of the world. I couldn't allow this to go on any longer. I had to be the destroyer of the world, or the world would have destroyed me. I had to be the one to get through to Jared or his end would be near. In the end, I want you to know that I do love. I love everything fully but it isn't enough to love something. It's not enough to love a world that is so broken with corruption.

My love, my blood, protect your heart from the cruelty of this world. Shelter yourself from the new world I have created. The world I create won't be anything you want. It will be full of heartache, like the heartache this world has created in me for years.

I know I shouldn't blame anyone, but I blame human kind. I blame the unkind words they said to me as a child. I blame the dirty looks I acquired on a daily basis. I blame the world for turning my insides vile and brutal.

I am the man who loved so deeply beyond words before they ruined me. Just as I loved humanity before it destroyed me.

I know you wanted to ask me if I was evil. I am. I am as evil as the world made me. I am a product of my environment. I am corruption's son. I am devastation's leader.

Forever and eternally,
Alec

Acknowledgements

Thank you to **my mom, my dad, Dina, Dimitri, Grandma, Susie, Great Grandmother and Yiayia** for giving me with the courage to write this book. I have many people to thank for the courage I have now.

I want to thank **Edee** for being patient with me, and helping me in so many different aspects of my life.

Thank you, **Christian,** for taking my pictures, and being one of the greatest people I know.

Thank you, **Patchwork Press,** for being my publishing home and welcoming me in so many ways.

Thank you, **Brittany,** for always being a great friend to me. You're always asking about Corruption, and you've waited patiently. I promise I won't ever say, "I let out the breath I didn't know I was holding."

Thank you to my **family** for always listening to me and encouraging me when it comes to writing. I love you all.

To my **mom**, I could write you a whole book of why I appreciate you. Thank you. Thank you. Thank you. For always believing in me, no matter what. I love you.

To my **dad**, thanks for always listening to me when things go wrong. I love you.

To **Dimitri**, I have two words for you, and those two words are: Delicate Crunch (lol). Love you, silly.

To **Dina**, We may not share a last name anymore, but you are forever my favorite, Mrs. Parker. You'll always be my best friend, my sister, my number one since day one. I love you.

To **Blackie,** I love you and miss you. This was my miniature schnauzer that made my life ten times better, and passed away this year. I never start my morning without saying hello to your ashes in passing.

To **Dobby,** my new puppy, who almost didn't make this possible with his neediness (lol). I still love you though.

To **Grandma and Great Grandmother,** I know you're both causing a ruckus in heaven as we speak. Love you two.

Finally, **thank you** for sticking with me throughout the trilogy. This isn't the end for me, and it's all because of you.

About the Author

Taylor Hondos obtained an English degree from the University of North Carolina at Greensboro in 2017. In high school, she began writing "Antidote" and finished writing it by the end of her freshman year of college. "Corruption" is the third and final book in the Antidote trilogy. She plans to release many books in 2018. She lives with her family in North Carolina.

www.ingramcontent.com/pod-product-compliance
Lightning Source LLC
Chambersburg PA
CBHW051459170626
46811CB00002B/554